Little Soldier

BERNARD ASHLEY

I should like to thank the Hon. Joyce Mpanga MP and Fred Kisembo, Esi Eshun, Denise Hyland and Tate and Lyle's Michael Grier for their help in my research.

ORCHARD BOOKS
96 Leonard Street, London EC2A 4XD
Orchard Books Australia
14 Mars Road, Lane Cove, NSW 2066
First published in Great Britain in 1999
Paperback original

A CIP catalogue record for this book is available from the British Library.
ISBN 1 86039 879 0
5 7 9 10 8 6
Printed in Great Britain

Little Soldier

BERNARD ASHLEY

CHAPTER ONE

'Here, man, come an' have a deck at the hole in Ken's arm. Show 'em your arm, Ken!' Theo Julien was trying to work up a crowd in the school yard like a market-stall man in Thames Reach - with Kaninda Bulumba his stock-in-trade. 'Come on, Ken, give 'em a show!'

But Kaninda's eyes said 'No! Get off! Don't touch!' The healed-over bullet hole in his arm wasn't there for using like street kids would, begging for shillings. It wasn't there for stares and chicken clucks. This hard little pit which his fingers kept finding in the night was what he'd got away with when the bullet holes in his family had done much worse and killed them. Over and over.

'Be more of a giggle seeing what other 'oles he's got!'

'I'm in for that crack!'

'Erk!'

'Seen his arm,' someone said. 'Seen it in PE. My mum done worse to my uncle...'

Theo grabbed at Kaninda walking away. 'Don't blow me out – only trying to make 'em feel sorry, man. Bleed for you.'

'Don't want bleeding, you got me?'

Theo clapped him on the back, Mr Broad-grin Bigheart. 'No? What you want, then, Ken?' He'd lost the punters.

Kaninda said nothing. He looked up at the school roof, at the steep angle of the satellite dish which told him the same thing every day – how far away from home he was, where the dish of the Nile Hotel sat as flat as a posho bowl. If he knew the angle of this one he could work out the miles. If he knew the maths.

He came back to Theo, growled. 'What I want? My land, and kill Yusulu killers.'

And Theo Julien had to go along with that.

Kaninda clutched his pet chameleon tight under his chest, wasn't going to let go ever, not in this world or the next. He tried to make his mind go as dark as the night outside, tried to think of nothing, be *dead. If the government soldiers came back through the door they didn't have to see any life in here, man or animal – nor pick up the tick of any thinking going on. When the Yusulu left a district dead, they left it dead – dead down to the last flat sack of a dog's body. Kaninda had to lie as still as a corpse, share the wet mud of his family's blood on the floor, pant in mosquito breaths, take no notice of the burning in his arm where he'd been hit by the bullet coming through his mother's belly – and pray to God the soldiers were too fired up with killing to burn down the house.*

'Is your seat belt fastened?'

The steward in his uniform was leaning across the woman to check. His pinky-white face pulled Kaninda back from where he'd been, and the chameleon against his chest became his own tight fist.

'It's morning. We're landing soon. Shall I open this?'

The man didn't wait for a yes or a no – as if he knew what was best for refugees. He slid up the light shield on the window.

'That's better,' the woman with Kaninda said, 'now we can see where we're going an' all.'

But Kaninda couldn't. All he could see were the rolling tops of the clouds like miles of up-country scrub, dyed pink by the rising sun: the colour of blood wetting a dress.

The steward went away, checking on others who were waking from their sitting-up sleep, those other kids brought out of the camp at Bikoto. *The lucky ones* , as they kept being told. Kaninda slewed his eyes for a look at this woman next to him, Captain Betty Rose. Big, not so black as him, sitting up in her seat like a teacher for a school photograph, going along obediently with the aeroplane orders for coming down out of the sky.

'Cabin crew – positions for landing.'

Captain Betty Rose patted Kaninda's knee as the plane went down into the mash of the clouds. 'Not long now, boy. Here comes London, an' your new home.' But her smile was directed up at the sky, not at him.

Kaninda shuffled the blanket on his lap; and beneath it he found the seat belt buckle and unfastened it. His eyes were slits, his mouth was dry closed. His life was finished. He didn't care what happened. If the plane crashed he *wanted* to die. He hoped it would. But he would never do what these people said. He took no orders from them or from anyone. His orders came from The Leopard – Colonel Munyankindi – and Sergeant Matu; from soldiers in the rebel army – to lie still, to fill plastics from puddles, to collect goa beans, to stand guard, to shoot and kill. The only other orders Kaninda Bulumba obeyed were given by himself. And the big one, if the aeroplane did not crash, was to turn round, go back and join up again with the Kibu rebels and help them do to the President and his Yusulu clansmen what they had done to his mother and his father and his little sister Gifty. A thousand times over.

At Heathrow Laura Rose stood waiting with her father for the flight to come in. *Landed* it had said on the screen; now they had to wait for the God's Force party to clear Immigration and come through with the orphans and their baggage. And as a welcome in case the press were there, Laura and the rest were in their red and gold uniforms; red for the blood of Christ and gold for the gates of heaven. With black lacy mini-briefs underneath for the rebel way she was thinking these days. Where Jesus couldn't see – and wouldn't look if He could.

Her dad put his arm round her epaulettes. 'Good to see her down safe, eh?'

'Yeah. Excellent.'

'No more chips!'

'And no more peace.'

Her dad backed off. 'She ain't that bad!'

'Not her. The boy. Kaninda. My new *brother*. God knows what we've got there.'

'Whatever we've got, he's had a terrible time. Left for dead when his family was massacred. No living soul in the world to love him. It's small enough sacrifice to make.'

Laura looked up at her dad, only a lieutenant while her mum was a captain and a minister. He always *said* the right thing, but it never came out as if he believed it with all his heart and all his soul. His prayers probably ran out of push halfway up to Heaven, while you bet her mum's got there on fast track.

But there was no fast track about coming through the airport gates. Everyone else from the flight came past and then there was a long wait with nothing happening.

'Were they on it?'

'Immigration,' Laura's dad told her. '"Asylum seekers" – loads of paperwork...'

And when they did come through, Laura's mother seemed to be holding it all in her hand, sheaves of it, flapping the refugee children on, six blank-faced kids dressed in white and grey. But Captain Betty Rose big and smiling. 'Hallelujah!' she called. 'God be praised indeed!' – even before she said *Peter* or *Laura*. All the same, the hug she gave to her daughter was a drop-everything affair.

Which Kaninda watched, kicking the trolley wheels.

'This is Kaninda.' All around them Monis and Mangengas and Nanous were being introduced to their new God's Force brothers and sisters, the rescue project completed, praise the Lord.

Or just started. Kaninda stood as still as a slave being inspected for use in the home. Peter Rose had to lift the boy's hand to shake it. Laura said 'Hi' but the boy stayed silent. And to get on with life the way life had to be got on with, Captain Betty led the contingent through Terminal One to where the God's Force minibus was waiting in Short Term Parking.

A white minibus, fourteen seater. The same sort of carrier that used to race the streets of Lasai City picking up passengers for work or market, the driver shouting the route – before the President's clansmen commandeered them, when what came out of the windows were bullets to clear the crowd.

It was still early morning in Britain, and three hours back on the clock. What was 9.00 a.m. Lasai time was 6.00 a.m. London, so the road into the capital was clear. And this was a road without potholes, where even the side streets were tarmac instead of rutted red earth – the big buildings not much different to Lasai City except for no shell holes, and the housing blocks and small shops neater and going on and on and on.

Kaninda leaned his head against the window and when it bumped against the glass he let it bump, let it hurt, bad as it liked. Because these roads were never where he wanted to be. This was all just the dog luck of being separated from the Kibu rebels and getting rounded up with stupid soft refugees.

It was the river. Uebe. Rivers were water, were drink and food, were a wash. They were roads, too, but on the attack orj on the run, rivers were sometimes dividers that had to be crossed.

Their force led by Sergeant Matu had come far up country to gather with The Leopard and the main rebel army at Kibu. Their guerrilla attacks on government patrols and their ambushes on troops were only flea bites on the mangy dog, but now the army was joining up to start the liberation. Radio messages, talk in the villages, leaflets on the road, they all told in secret code what the squads had to do. Head north. Assemble. So days were spent on the trek, pushing through sedge and flooding; sleeping under guard in the thatched huts of far villages; hiding up in the markets and small towns when the government lorries came shooting through. Because the rebels' day was going to come.

And everything was going well – till a traitor or a tortured prisoner spilled something he shouldn't spill, and a platoon of government soldiers got onto the tail of Sergeant Matu's men – good trackers and with helicopter help. Rotors flattening the bamboo, Kaninda had to dive off the track and sink himself neck deep in a narrow channel of the Uebe: saving himself, but losing the rest, and good luck for him, too, because the killing was soon over with bullets to waste, and Sergeant Matu and the rest would never make the rendezvous, not in this world. But risking the crocs and swimming the river, Kaninda took the wrong turn, into the sun instead of away from it, and going through one village too many he found himself in the saving hands of the Red Cross. No gun. No bullets. No story, except the lie that after the shooting-up of his home he'd wandered and wandered in a dizzy state and kept himself alive by thieving. While the hole in his arm had healed itself.

No, he did not want to be here. Not in London, not at this house where the carrier was stopping, where this Mrs Captain Betty Rose was looking at the building and giving off another 'Hallelujah!'

The place was like many he'd passed on the road

from the airport. It was joined to the houses on both sides, going up to second windows like something in the centre of Lasai City. And it was grey, dull, *dingy*, and a world away from his war. It was not like their house had been outside the city, plot number 14, Bulanda Road, one floor, painted white with the first halfmetre in ochre so the splashing of the heavy rains didn't throw earth stains up the walls: cement paint all bright in the sun; till it was suddenly death bright with blood all over it where the goat and the dogs were shot.

They got out of the carrier. Captain Rose's man was going on somewhere with the other people who had ridden with them: two stupid refugee girls in white shirts who had not said a word since Bikoto, and another boy, younger than Kaninda. And no words needed now, as Kaninda followed into the house, not carrying anything because he had nothing to carry. There was just him, and he was too much.

He trailed inside, into a narrow passage, where the woman looked all round like inspection time. He stood turbulent just inside the door, wanted to run at that wall with his head and smash himself to the next world.

'Come on,' said the girl. 'Your room's up here.'

Kaninda followed, looking at his shoes as his feet

felt the soft of all the furry matting on the floor.

'Carpet,' she told him. 'Is that new to you?'

So? It was, after weeks of dry track, wet track, grass and mud, when the first proper concrete floor he'd stepped on had been at the airport; the first under his feet since that bloody night at home...

'Here you are. And, 'case you're wondering, I'm Laura.' The girl opened the door of a room just round from the top of the stairs. 'Bathroom's back there.'

Kaninda went on past her into his room.

'Hope you like it. Hope you're happy here.'

He slammed the door.

But it wasn't two minutes before it was bustled open – time only for a stare at the window.

'So, Kaninda, how you like your room? Pretty com-*for*table, eh?' The woman had come direct in. Even his own mother used to shout, 'Open!'

'You got a cupboard here for hanging up your clothes, an' a chest-of-drawers for your underwear and socks, and here by your bed's a Bible. And the bathroom's—'

'Seen.'

'Good.' She stood facing him, took up all the space between him and the door. 'Now we got to settle what you're going to call us...'

Kaninda turned away and looked out of the

window; shut her out. Over and between roofs, he could see a river.

'I'll give you some things to choose from. *Cap'n Rose* – is who I am. *Aunt Betty* , or *Tante Betty,* is what some family people call me. Or, I don't mind – I'd like – please the Lord – Social Services an' the judge giving us their blessing – if you picked on calling me what Laura does.' There was a long space with just the breathing going on. 'Which goes by Mum.'

Still just the breathing, and the look from Kaninda continuing at the river and the funnels of a ship.

'Eh? What you think?'

Somehow he kept the pin in his grenade, thought of Sergeant Matu's orders – the orders he'd been obeying since he'd fallen into the hands of the Red Cross. *'If you're taken, lie low, submissive as a cringing dog, an' wait the chance, an' when you can, run!* run! *You got me?'*

'Well, something'll come. "Patience is a pain, but it pays." Peter – he's put you some things in your wardrobe. You have a look. Then we're going to have a proper English breakfast. I'll get Laura to give you a call an' all.'

She went, and Kaninda stayed fixed on the river. *Fix on something outside the cell.* And he knew his geography from Social Studies at school. He knew that all the rivers of the world joined up with all the seas; and all the waters of all the seas joined up along all the coasts of all the countries. Which meant East Africa, too, joined with the sea along the white sand beaches and at the ports where they sent out the sugar and the coffee.

Not being a bird he couldn't be joined by the air, the way they'd come. But the sea, that was different. Ships, boats, they could join things up.

He looked down at his bony arms, getting to look like a famine boy's, the scarred hole gone dead in colour. And he asked himself, could he eat enough of this woman's food to give him the strength to row halfway round the world? Because if hate and anger were strength he could do it, just.

The other side of the bedroom wall, Laura was taking off her God's Force uniform having shown the flag of Christ; not that anyone at Heathrow had taken the least bit of notice. *Hallej-bloody-luyah!*

She looked at herself in the mirror, the underneath her. She was pale, more of her father's white than her mother's Seychelles gold, and not bad for thirteen on the figure front.

'Laura!'

And throwing the black briefs behind the bed

before the door could get flung open.

'Yeah?'

'Call Kaninda for his breakfast, will you?'

She pulled a face at the mirror. *Kaninda!* She was going to wish the sound of that name a lot further off before she was too much older. Like the name of *God's Force*. There was more wrong with life than right, and that was the truth of it.

But she went, and knocked on the boy's door; not expecting, and definitely not getting, any reply.

CHAPTER TWO

To everyone around, Theo Julien was a right laugh. He could slaughter the kids, crack a smile from Old Bill, get a giggle off the school bursar. And in the way a stand-up's at home on a pub platform, his space was The Front on the Barrier Estate.

The Barrier Estate – a mile downstream from the Thames Barrier, and The Front – a paved area among the flats, three sides of building and one side open to the river through the railings. Walkway, car park, playground, lovers' lane, drug push, home base to the Barrier Crew, everything to everyone, this was where the life went on. And Theo never without an audience, if it was only seagulls.

It was Saturday afternoon and his big brother Mal was working on a Ford Escort he'd got hold of. At least, Lydia his girlfriend was, Mal was holding the toolbag and fumbling out what she shouted for.

Handy as a pair of boxing gloves, was Mal. And Theo was doing his thing, sitting on a wall, a streak of human graffiti keeping up the crack for the kids who hung about, the Crew wannabes.

''E was after a Rover but the guy was still sittin' in it.'

Mal reacted. 'This is my car, man, sho' 'nuff.'

'Bloke *wanted* this nicked. Ford Escort! *Real cool!'*

The kids laughed, and the biggest, Sharon, flicked her hand like 'no hope!'

'Nicked *nuthin'*, said Mal, 'it's *my* car, le-gal: what're you tellin' these people?'

Lydia came out from under. 'Cut the crap both of yous an' take them number plates off,' she ordered. 'Be a bit useful.'

'See, she's ringing it.'

'Ding dong!' said Sharon.

'We're doin' it up. *Cleanin'* it. Don' want a shinin' red lim an' plates all shot up with grease. I'm gonna strip that off an' paint them over.'

Theo came down off the wall. 'You wanna keep them plates, Lyd, an' swap the car! Be favourite.' But while Mal unscrewed the front end, Theo made himself useful as asked and unscrewed the back. Then he went for a spit in the river and a watch of the fleck as it drifted upstream. He looked out across the wide flat of the water to the Tate and Lyle Refinery where a ship was having its cargo sucked from the holds, while a scoop dredger cleared the silt to give deep enough water; the clank of it some sort of theme tune for south London. When it stopped people thought they were living somewhere else. For a bit.

Which was not the case for Theo. After his father disappeared the year before – without even remembering a bloom for Theo's mother's grave – Theo came to live with his brother Mal, and acted like he knew where he was every minute of the day. Refugees do, they're always on the watch for not being wanted.

But who was this dancing through the bollards towards Theo with a smile like headlights through fog?

'Laura! Wotcha Lor!'

There was no one else about. Mal and Lyd had gone in for a bite, and Sharon and the kids had drifted off a way.

'Hi-ya!' Laura looked at this jive as he fidgeted and tapped. 'Give us a breath of this air!'

'Wha' for?' Theo turned with her to stand leaning on the rail, sucking in the sour salt of the Thames.

'He's come!'

'Jesus? At last?'

'No, an' don't blaspheme. The Lasai kid. Kaninda.'

'Kan-in-dah! Why, what's your prob with him?'

'None.' Laura shrugged. 'And everything.'

'Ah! Am I s'posed to catch on to that?'

'Well, he's...I don't know...' She slipped an arm through Theo's; wouldn't have done it along her street, but down here was two main roads away from home and the kids weren't looking – they were talking sex or something in a huddle. ''Course, it might not be him at all. Could be me.'

'*Could* be! Got to be. Lor, you got more lump than porridge these days!'

'Well...' Laura wasn't ready to talk about it. How did she share her falling out with God, her wanting to go against everything her mother and father stood for? It wasn't like chewing over the state of Miss Rivers' hair or the stains on Mr Cheff.

Theo came out from holding arms and faced her. 'You want Paris or Atlanta?'

'*What*?'

'You're actin' *terminal*. So what Disneyland you wanna go to?'

Laura shook her head at this terrible taste.

'You need a rush of some sort, girl. An' I don't mean 'puff' or 'trips'. Some *Sega-world* skin peeler, you want. Or I tell you, you're gonna turn sour as ol' puss's milk!'

When you went to the edge by being friends with someone your mum had chucked out of the Junior Force, you had to play his game – or else why go to the edge? 'So, what you got in mind?' Laura wanted to know: 'The Barrier run?'

The Barrier run was the initiation. Laura knew that getting into the Crew – real credibility – you had to run along the river rail at low tide, fast stepping over thirty-six round blue bosses, with a drop to the strand of thirty feet. And you did a hundred metres of this in less than half a minute. Theo was in, but Laura hadn't dared; not even practised at high water.

'Nah. Suthink out of the run o' stuff...'

They turned their backs on the river – the clanking, and the blow off the water, the smell and the lap of high tide up the watergate steps. It was April with the chill off, and when the sun was on it even the Barrier Estate looked a fair old place to live.

And better than Wilson Road right now, Laura thought, with this Kaninda moping in his room and her dad being given the full tale of God's work in Lasai. It was only mad Theo who was keeping her sane these days: off the wall Theo who stood for everything her mother wouldn't like.

'You wanna be a devil now and then! Cut yourself out of that holy skin! Be a bit *sool.*'

'Sool?'

'Grabbin'. Gettin' hold o' life. Sool.'

'You reckon?'

They wandered sideways, edgeways, stepping on each other's toes over to where the Escort was reflecting the sun off a wet bonnet, standing in a scum of suds.

'Mal's wheels.'

'Yeah?' Laura rarely went potty over plastic and metal and rubber. But for something to do she took an interest in the car, bent to look at the dashboard since that's what people did. 'Are these car keys s'posed to be in here?'

'Good ol' Mal! Cementhead!'

Laura turned away, she'd had a look and done her duty. But that wasn't good enough for Theo.

'Let's have a sit in,' he said. He looked up at the balconies looking down. 'A bit private...'

When you were sent for a packet of sugar you went for it fast – if your mother was Dolly Hedge's mother. You got it on credit, no refusal, and you got it back home before the kettle boiled. And watch out, Babe, if you've let anyone get in your way.

But then there was Queen Max, big Maxine Bendix who ran the local Ropeyard streets, and no one got out of her way if she wanted a word.

'Little Dolly!'

'Wha'?'

Max was done up, hair in a high tuft, tight orange vest, all arms, bluebird tattoo on her shoulder. Waiting for someone, but it couldn't have been Dolly; the little girl hadn't known she was coming herself.

'Where you goin'?'

'Shop.'

Dolly tried to pass by Max on the pavement but with those legs sticking out from where she was sat on the low wall it would have meant going into the road.

'What you getting?'

'Sugar.'

'Payin'?'

'Nah.'

'Get us a Twix, then.'

A Twix; and not a request but an order. Nothing illegal by age, not fags or booze, but it would go down in the book against Rene Hedges' name; and if Rene Hedges spotted it, it would look like Dolly was having one over her.

All the same, no one said no to Maxine Bendix.

'I'll try.'

Max pulled in her long legs; but stuck one out again and lifted Dolly on a boot as she passed, up the crutch, in the air. 'Try hard! I'll be here!'

'Yeah.'

She let Dolly go, who went scurrying along towards Patel's News, but with her eyes all round her as if she were working out back ways home.

'Sad car!' Theo was sitting in the driver's seat like a customer on a car lot. 'I mean, *Ford Escort*!'

Laura really wasn't interested. Really. 'It's a car. If it goes, it goes. It gets you about. If it doesn't, one load of tin's the same as the next load of tin.'

Theo shook his head. 'Give me a Tornado that don't go, over a Ford Escort that don't go – any day.'

'What, to look at?'

'To reckon myself in. See, with a Tornado your arms are out full stretch like Indianapolis Five Thousand racing, an' you're right down here—' he slid his backside forward, lowered himself till it was just his eyes above the level of the dashboard, growled a meaty engine noise.

Laura sat watching him as he steered the slack of the wheel round some imaginary California curves.

'Raaaaar... C'mon,' – he drove one-handed as he

pressed her shoulder down – 'get on the freeway to LA.'

'I wish!' And Laura played Theo's game, slid down next to him till their eyes were level; her skirt riding up, but leaving it.

'Raaaaar! Route Maribou to the old Cayoo!' Theo was away in his head now.

'What's that mean?'

'Dunno. Nuthink. Sounds the stuff, though.' And he roared them into a left and a right with a slick gear change in the air, raa-ing up an octave. Except, instead of going back to two hands on the wheel he did one more gear change – onto Laura's leg, just above the knee – and left his hand there.

'Raaaaar.' Lower in his throat.

Laura gave him a look, could tell he knew what was coming next – her giving his cheeky hand the brush off. No way would he think he could stay holding her leg. Like, no way would her mother think her little soldier Laura could go cold on God's Force and all its good works... So she didn't brush Theo off, not straight away; she said nothing, did nothing, stared out of the windscreen down Route Maribou to the old Cayoo. Rebel thoughts.

Which seemed all too much for Theo; as if letting his hand stay there was asking the question of what did he do next?

'Raaaaar.' And like a cook on a hot tin Theo jumped his hand off her leg back onto the steering wheel, and for something to do with his right, dropped it to twist the key in the ignition, starting the engine. For real.

'Theo!'

''S'all right, we're on The Front, it ain't a public road...'

There was no one about; the kids had gone off to annoy elsewhere. Theo pulled down an imaginary pair of sunglasses, put the car into third gear, let out the clutch, and took it in a tight lock around the Barrier paving. And in the rebel mood she was in, Laura said nothing, breathed in sharp at the sudden feel of danger, and with her skirt still riding high, let Theo drive where he wanted.

Dolly Hedges ran out of the shop with the sugar, looking to find a clever way home. Just the sugar, no Twix. She'd rather get a smack from Queen Max than a punch from her mum.

The Ropeyard Street Estate was a sad part of south London, half old houses, half sixties' flats, built on a clearance job started by Adolf Hitler: shops with steel shutters for windows, pubs with no food, dogs on the lope, and police cars that only ever drove through with blue lights flashing. And never mind God looking down, it was more likely to be the Metropolitan Police helicopter. Where the Barrier Estate had been built with civic hope, the Ropeyard was all tight streets, bald grass mounds, and sad faces – a place where a Twix bar could make someone's day. Saturday afternoon, racing on the pub telly, Queen Max waiting for anyone to come along who'd offer some cash for a favour, and this small girl getting sugar home to her tea-addict mother; needing to take a diversion round those long legs stuck out across the pavement, which meant a cut across Ropeyard Street to the street where she lived.

A small packet of sugar squeezed in a tight fist, a look left, a look right for danger – not up and down the road, but along the pavement for the sight of Queen Max coming grabbing round a corner. And, all clear for a bit, so – go!

Into a road which wasn't empty, always one or two speeding down there, and crack!

Dolly Hedges was in a heap in the gutter next to a scatter of white sugar like crematorium ash; with Queen Max coming steaming too late round a corner to the sound of a scream. A hard stare at a red car squealing off and then a lift of the small, still head. And others came, too, brought out by the sounds of an accident.

'Little Dolly.'

'Poor cow.'

'She all right?'

'She look all right?!' Queen Max cradled the girl's head.

'Is she alive?'

'Dunno.'

'What's that all over her?'

'Sugar.'

'Looks like coke.'

'You wish. Keep her still.'

'Anyone phoned the ambulance?'

A kid with a mobile started to tap the 999.

'And tell 'em Police an' all,' Queen Max said. 'Tell 'em, hit and run, red car, no plates.'

Everyone was busy, wanting to help with this still bundle of scrappy clothes lying there in the gutter.

'Who's goin' to tell Rene Hedges?' someone asked.

But nobody volunteered to do that.

CHAPTER THREE

Kaninda walked away from the blood and the bodies, cold shock shaking him in the heat of the sun. He'd plugged his arm, wound a headscarf of his mother's round it tight. He swayed across the grass and stumbled through the gap in the hedge, the way the soldiers had come cutting in – the steel gates still locked and useless. Smoke hazed over the city centre where buildings had been torched. Staring through wide dry eyes, Kaninda held his suffocated chameleon to his stomach and headed the other way because that was where the others were walking – a string of scared Kibu families on the road, their things balanced in bundles on their heads and slung over their pushed bicycles, trekking together to get away from the Yusulu.

There was nothing left for Kaninda at 14 Bulunda Road: no mother, no father, no sister, no place to live, no life. *He either went on standing still, shaking; or he walked round in circles; or he stood and shouted his head off, screamed for the soldiers to come back and put bullets and machetes into him, too.*

In the end he'd walked away from the bodies because they weren't anyone any more. Their faces weren't the people he loved, weren't who they'd been – even little Gifty wasn't herself, lying twisted and torn after she'd hit the wall and slid down like a terrible road death. There was no kissing them goodbye – there was nowhere to put his lips. It was get out fast and leave the dogs and rats and flies to do the work of the spade.

Finally, howling was what Kaninda did. His head back, he howled like a wounded wolf. And none of the others on the march gave a blink to his pain. They all had their own to carry.

It was like a cocoon to Kaninda, the room at the front of the Rose's house. Everything was soft, he wanted to tear it with his nails, bite at it; the woolly floor, the pulpy paper on the walls, the curtains like bedcovers, the feathery flowers in the fireplace, the cushions and the padded footstool. The lounger at home had been stiff cane, and he and Gifty had had to sit straight-backed on hard chairs. The sharp cornered table was in the middle of the room, the walls were rendered plaster, and the concrete floor had paper-thin mats of dyed palm strips on it. If you fell over at home you injured yourself more indoors than you did out, where the grass and the red earth were soft. In this room here you could throw yourself around like a prisoner going mad and never get hurt: but he was desperate to try.

'This is your home, go where you want, make it yours,' Mrs Captain Betty Rose had commanded. 'You've come a long way an' all, but the longest way round is the shortest way home.' And she'd left him to it while she got on with telling her tale of God's work in Lasai to the lieutenant. But the controlled part of Kaninda's mind as he sat and stared at the dust in a sunbeam, specks drifting slow or falling fast, was out of this house and over to where the river ran. The house, London, England, they were punishment for being caught; but different manoeuvres went at different speeds; he was going to have to obey Sergeant Matu and lie still in cover a while and wait.

He was so quiet on his own in the front room that it could have been empty, a safe haven for Laura to come into as she let herself into the house. The way to her room lay up the stairs past the door to the back where her mother was preaching to her father; and the door was open. She slid into the front room like a sinner into a confessional, waiting for the best moment to go upstairs.

But – 'You're quiet in here.'

Kaninda shrugged. The girl was out of breath, had that grey in her face like Gifty when she'd been sucking at the sugar. Sweet, dead Gifty, that face he saw in every sleep, his shaking nightmare. He moved to go out, to get to his bed, any place on his own. But Laura didn't move from the doorway to let him, so he stood and stared at the heave of her chest, looked away at the flocky wall. She was troubled, but so?

'You know pain, Kaninda, don't you?'

He screamed in his head, but said nothing.

'You've been torn about inside.'

Her words were like her laying hands on him; but he didn't want her healing hands. What did she know of what he'd lost, what he'd seen, what he'd *done* – and what he ached to do again when he could get back home to do it? *The longest way round is the shortest way home*. So, Mrs Captain Betty Rose, is halfway round the world long enough?

'Show the river?' Just about the first words Kaninda had spoken to Laura. Something to break him out of this cocoon.

'Did you know that's where I've been? You've not been following me?'

Kaninda closed his eyes in a long blink of denial. But instead of refusing him, the girl suddenly seemed to think it was a good idea. She shouted through to the back room and took him out of the house, walked him slowly through the streets to the river, calling to some smaller kids on the way, like showing him off.

It was hard under his feet, outside. Everywhere here was slab stone. The beaten earth of the Lasai streets kicked up dust, but they gave bounce to the feet. The sun had lost any heat it had, and lack of sleep on the flight began to put heaviness in Kaninda's step; but he was used to the sun going down on him marching, and he was used to being tired. When there was a target everything else held its breath till you'd hit it; and he would always keep going till he hit and hit and hit. The target here was the river; the Thames: this was what he wanted to see. But, hard buildings and concrete walkways up to the bank, words and scrawlings painted all over, ironwork along the edge and steps down to the water, just a few weedy trees growing out of the bricks to give any vegetation – this Thames was nothing like the Uebe. It was water, though, part of the world's rivers and seas, somehow joined with

Lasai. It was hope; and what he wanted in his hate and anger was some hope.

'You great div, where's them plates?'

There was fuss and bother going on as loud as someone getting the glasses snatched off their face by a street kid. A pretty woman was shouting at a man who looked as if he'd let the goats into the beans. Both black, her dressed manly in a grey tracksuit, looked as if she could do him some hurt if she wanted. He was looking as if she could, too, because he kept a red car positioned between the two of them, whether she came at him this direction or that.

'I dunno, do I? I put them on that wall, 'sho'nuff.'

But on that wall sat a boy who was keeping himself out of things, who lifted himself to show there was nothing under his backside except the concrete.

'An' I s'pose them numbers just took off on their own! Went to find another car to screw theirself onto!'

The boy on the wall looked at Laura, flapped a hand and said 'Hi!' in a weak voice.

Laura stepped into things. 'Malcolm, Lydia, this is Kaninda. He's living with us. From Lasai.' It was like she was trying to douse the fire burning these two.

'You ain't seen no number plates?' the woman asked them both.

Laura shook her head. Kaninda looked at the car and saw where they ought to be, blank spaces on the front and the back of the vehicle. Number plates gave cars away. The Lasai boys knew which plates meant money, and which meant government cars – the plates with the G in front – so no one robbed them or they'd be chased and shot for sure. The soldiers never bothered about the others.

'Theo...'

'Laura, how you doin'?' The boy slid down off the wall. 'Long time, no see...'

'I'm all right. This is—'

'You said. All right, Ken?'

It was the river Kaninda wanted, just a look at it to make himself more content, check it *was* water and not a mirage.

'Jesus, Mal, it's *hot*!' The tracksuit woman had leaned on the car bonnet. 'This engine's hot. You been running it up?'

Now the man Mal joined in the outrage. 'Not since I brung it, s'morning. Someone's been in this!'

''Cos you only left the stupid keys in it!' She grabbed them out of the ignition. 'I'm gonna eat 'em!' But instead of in her mouth she shoved them in a tracksuit pocket. 'Ain't you got no sense, Mal Julien?'

'No.' But he was shaking his head at a couple of questions back. 'Theo, you know anything 'bout this?'

'No, man. No way. Been off along The Front, me.' But the boy's face had the look of a man who'd been stealing rations, who was going to get a rifle butt if he showed the truth. 'There was some kids about, but I never knowed you'd left the keys in...' He suddenly gave a whoop, as if he was crucified by the laugh of it. 'You must've promised him a real hot dinner, Lyd, mekin' him leave his car plates on the wall an' his keys in the dash. Somethink spicy!'

'*Our* plates! *Our* keys! An' what he had was cold – nothin' like hot as the box comin' round your ears...' And the woman ran at Theo, was going to dish out punishment to him.

But Theo was off the mark, away like a waterbuck up river with Laura following, so Kaninda had to go. After the woman had given up, the three of them stopped by two ornamental cannons and looked back to watch her reversing the car into the lock-up; but Laura and Theo were acting like two people scratching the same rash; they just kept on looking at one another.

Kaninda left them to whatever their secret was. So? He turned away and stared out at the river.

The other side of the water was more the sort of sight he knew from going to Lasai Port; where it was built up along the stretch of the riverside with buildings, with pipes up into the air and big round containers. But he wasn't interested in that; because between here and there was the water, the flat water, all the same level around the world. Like a road, his *connection*, a link with home. And he suddenly felt so far away, so sad and twisted, just, that he would have cried if tears had not been long dried out of him. Dried by the guilt of being alive.

Dolly Hedges lay like a sacrifice. Intensive Care beds are not for sleeping in but for being worked on at a comfortable height by the medics; high, with room underneath for oxygen cylinders and drainage bottles, and all the equipment of life-saving. No one looks comfortable in Intensive Care because comfort isn't what they're about. Visitors don't sit, they stand, and they skip out of the way for crucial bits of business to be done.

Rene Hedges was there with a polystyrene cup of sweet tea; sunken eyes, a ring in her nose, watching every slight coma breath of the small girl as if she were counting them. A policewoman hovered a step or so further back, with Queen Max giving her the word.

'Red car, didn't see no plates.'

'You didn't see plates, or the car didn't have them?'

'Didn't see 'em.' Max looked at the still girl, and back at the notebook in the policewoman's hand. 'No, don't put that. It didn't have no plates 'cos I look at plates. You c'n reckon people by plates.'

'What people?'

Max stared at the policewoman. 'People. Poncy lettering. Their own initials. But she said suthink...'

'The girl?'

'This one. Little Dolly. When I knew she was alive.'

'And what did she say?'

'She said, "White." Yeah, that's what she said.'

'White?'

'White.'

'What do you think she meant by that – if it was a red car?'

You could search Queen Max. 'Ask her when she wakes up. I don't know, do I?'

The policewoman nodded, closed her notebook, whispered again. 'Thanks for your help.'

'Yeah.'

Rene stopped a nurse who was going away with

a strip of printout. 'She is gonna wake up, in't she, mate?'

The nurse smiled, waved the strip of paper. 'We'll have to study all this, get the X-rays back. But she's holding her own at the moment.'

Rene looked at Dolly again, shook her head. 'Clumsy little cow—' in the softest, kindest of voices. 'All for my packet of sugar...' She looked round at the policewoman. 'But what I don' get is what she was doing crossing there. It's not the way she'd go. It's like she was keeping out of someone's way...'

'She'll tell us. And we'll find the car, Rene. Some joyrider. We'll see who's had a car nicked...'

'You do that.'

Queen Max had been looking the other way. Now she cut in to lay a hand on the policewoman's shoulder. 'Do us a favour, mate. Don' find it 'fore I do. Your justice ain't 'alf as good as mine!' And she stalked out of Intensive Care, definitely *going* somewhere.

CHAPTER FOUR

Sunday always meant God's Force in full voice: the same way that Monday nights meant Junior God's Force, Thursdays meant God's Force 'Silver Bells' band practice, and Saturdays could be a God's Force shopping mall prom or collecting clothes or printing the programmes for Sunday's God's Force meetings. Then it was Sunday again.

All hail the power of Jesu's name

Let angels prostrate fall...

THUMP!

No-one lost their place while Laura was on the bass drum. The God's Force headquarters in Clara Street rattled at its Chubb locks as Captain Betty scowled down at Laura in the band. *Too much!*

But Laura could keep the beat in her sleep, and her mind wasn't with them this morning.

And crown Him! THUMP.

Crown Him! THUMP.

Cro-own Him! THUMP.

Crown Him Lord of all! THUMP THUMP.

Laura was living yesterday's crucial seconds, which were repeating and repeating and repeating themselves in her head as if she might never move on, never grow any older. In fifty years' time she'd still be rooted in yesterday.

'It's easy, girl – if you can ride the dodgems, you can drive one of these babes. Right on in this gear, an' stamp down on that pedal if you gotta throw out the anchors...'

'This one?'

'You got it! Route Maribou to the old Cayoo!'

'So we praise You, Lord, for sendin' us to Lasai, with the eyes to see what we did see, an' the means to bring those unhappy children out...'

'Be praised!'

And it had all gone along OK for the girl who'd had enough of this blind faith and loud praise – sitting under age and rebellious at the wheel of Mal's and Lyd's car having a go at steering along Ropeyard Street...

'Massacre, gen-o-cide, disease an' orphanhood. The Lord picked us to pick them out and give them a fresh start in His name...'

'Be praised!'

'Be praised indeed!'

Till the van had come from nowhere, and like on the dodgems, instead of braking people swerve – and Theo had pushed over in a flash to grab the wheel: a bump, and off up the street and round the corner, out of sight of that something lying in the gutter...

'He guided us the way we should go, and He gave us the courage to bring those children out to safety.'

'Amen.'

'Amen, amen.'

'Amen indeed!'

Laura looked at her mother, glowing up there on the platform with the good she and the others had done. And deserving to feel righteous in a way, to be getting the public praise – but what Laura wished for was a Catholic confession box she could go into for the private word she needed, to tell a priest what a terrible thing she'd done. And her hand twitched with the impulse to put the stick clean through the skin of this God's Force drum.

There was a voice in her ear.

'Laura!'

And it wasn't her conscience. It was her father, coming white-faced round the door from the assembly room at the back of the percussion.

'Where's Kaninda?'

Laura shrugged. 'He was out there with you, waiting to be paraded...'

'Well, he's paraded off, that's all!'

The bandleader raised her hands, ready for the *Soldiers' March* while the collection plates went round. But it would be played without the bass drum because Laura had sidled out to go and look for the refugee runaway.

It was over a padlocked gate and down the green steps and Kaninda was under purple-ended branches growing out of cracks in the wall – the tidal river at low ebb with channels in the mud running out towards the sluggish flow. And across the river, some way from the bank at a deep water quay, sat a ship unloading. He narrowed his eyes at the reflection off the water, remembered the way he and the rebels had squinted through strips cut in tree bark to protect their sight and see better in bright light. He saw a big hose going down into the ship's hold, he saw the rust on the hull, and a flag hanging dead from the stern.

It was a big river, this; more like the Nile than the Uebe; and a lot wider than the Lasai River where his father had taken him. He squatted on the steps again. Who wanted to be marched onto a platform and stared at by Mrs Captain Betty Rose's church people? *Hallelujah! God be praised!* He had been paraded enough by these people – for feeding, for medicine, for measuring; for selection to come to this loud concrete country – when he should not be here, he should not be breathing. But since he was breathing, it should be the Kibu rebel air of sweat and gun oil, detonation and smoky explosion where bits of Yusulu bodies were left hanging in trees...

It was a warm April morning, and mixed in the angry churning of his stomach was a sadness at seeing this water, bringing back those private times with his father on an afternoon off from the mine offices: fishing for Nile perch and wrapping them in matoke leaves to bake them in the embers of a small fire – nothing sweeter. Except the being there with his father.

'Keep yourself from the side, boy. They see up the bank, fish, a twist of the water. They see you before you see them.' And after a lucky catch one day his father had slit the fish's belly, pointing with his knife at what the fish had eaten. 'Can you see these lily seeds? That's what he eats. That's what we'll bait his brothers with...'

And all that sort of talk; things his father's father had told him, now passing them on to Kaninda, clan lore. 'Leave that fish, he's got a parrot mouth. He's going to be poisonous.'

So what sort of things could a man like that Lieutenant Peter ever pass on to a child?

A small twin-engined jet suddenly came swooping down, across the river and over the ship. It roared like a Yusulu government fighter, the only plane in the Lasai sky, small and fierce – first the roar, and then the tear of rocket missiles. It had Kaninda ducking small, pressing himself in under the overhang of the weedy trees. But no rockets fired. This was London, not Lasai City or Kibu Province. It made him feel stupid, the ducking his head – like a kid who's just joined the rebels and thrown himself into the scrub at the sound of a breaking stick. Jumpy, scared of his own smell. If you were going to live, you learned to be lion-hearted very fast.

Parrot-mouthed fish! Puffed up. Like the comic pictures of Martin Nshamihigo, the Lasain president the Kibu hated, as if making him look funny could make him seem less evil. Nshamihigo of the Yusulu clan, the ruler of Lasai, the man who with his own hands tortured Kibu mineworkers found with diamonds in their cracks, having had his soldiers stick them there.

'Two clans, two peoples, one flag.' As an office manager in the Katonga mine, Kaninda's father

had said he always had to ride two bucking horses at once: one of the underdog Kibu clan, but the other of the Yusulu owners. And when the horses had taken different roads in the uprising, the man had been split into two, and the family split in pieces with him, except Kaninda.

Family. Clan. Tribe. Race. *Difference*. Kaninda's fingers went to the hard scar of the bullet hole in his right arm, one difference between him and these kids in England. That plane hadn't strafed; what would anyone here know about clan hatreds? The Yusulu and the Kibu: both Lasain, but each descended from different ancient kings. One king Ndahura, of the fertile lands, the agricultural clan. The other Cwa, the Kibu king, whose people were nomadic and traded in cattle – until an epidemic of cattle disease destroyed their herds and the Kibu were at the mercy of the Yusulu: who had met the English and discovered diamonds on their fertile land, and spared the Kibu to be their slaves, their mineworkers.

Kaninda looked at his shadow on the river steps. You could tell the difference between people. The northern Kibu taller, less flesh on their bones; the Yusulu from the centre and the south, smaller; these differences you saw first, even in the mixed marriages where it was some this, some that, and the clan they clung to was decided by the work they did. You were either Yusulu on top or Kibu underneath – until the horrific deaths when the Katonga Mine caved in and the Kibu decided they'd had enough...

A war was still to be won – and him not there to fight it. Now he crouched on the green steps, one knee up, could have had an M16 across his body. *Feet, grip, sights, breath, trigger, fire!* He wanted to blast a burst of fire across the world: but he could see only as far as that ship over there. He tried to make out the flag which was showing itself on a flutter of breeze a long way off; he thought he could see black, brown and green stripes, and some symbol in the middle. But the name on the ship's side was too rusted to see.

He shivered. It was suddenly colder, and turning dull now. In Lasai it was always the same except when the rains came. Here it was like one place one minute, another place the next. A sudden flash caught his eye, the sun reflecting on a swirl of water rippling over the shiny mud; like a fish in the shallows on a cool day, when the perch came in from out deep to bask in warmer waters.

But this wasn't any fish. This was something stiff and shiny, sticking up out of the mud. And those weren't scales or fins on it, but something else, something silver, precious looking, glittering like a swathe of diamond chips.

Kaninda took off his shoes – he didn't bother with wearing Mrs Captain Betty Rose's socks – rolled up his trouser legs and trod out into the sucking mud to see what it was. Slippery mud, the same the world over, but cold here, and oily. And in the way that water always catches you however careful you're being, the lap of the Thames had wet his trouser roll-ups before he could fish out the shiny thing he'd seen. So?

Nothing precious, but a number plate from a car.

The number plate? Was it the number plate those people had been jumping like arrow frogs about? He took a careful turn around – it's in changing direction that you lose your footing in the shallows, when the platoon always has a hand on the shoulder in front – and he sucked back into his dissolving footprints to get to the steps again where he washed the plate off with a wet tissue.

The Barrier Estate was Sunday morning lazy, which meant empty. It came more to life on Sunday afternoons when people started drifting out of their flats; mornings were for slack. And no one much ever came to see the estate for what they could see; people who wanted to see the river went out on launches from Greenwich Pier.

But today Queen Max had come to see the estate. Queen Max and two of the Ropeyard Road 'Federation', Charlie Ty and Snuff Bowditch. They were doing the walkways together, not skulking along but striding like combat troops on an operation, Queen Max well in the front and the other two side by side, eyes everywhere and mouths shut tight. Ask them a question and you'd get answered with a boot, or something heavy held in the hand.

They rode a lift to a top balcony, looked out between the leaves of a pensioner's potted plants.

'Nothink in *red*!' Snuff said. He was thin, bony, dirty, hard. His bitten nail jabbed down at the vehicles in front of the central block of flats. Parked up were all the colours cars had, but nothing red.

'You got a dodgy car, you gonna leave it out down there, son? Not having plates says it's nicked, so you stash it away, don' you?' Charlie Ty, tall for a Chinese, turned back off the balcony, stared out the pensioner who was wavering behind a net curtain. He scratched at his acne, showing the tattooed F on his right forearm. 'They've got it in a lock-up gettin' a respray, an't they?'

But Queen Max was shutting him up and pointing down at the riverside walk, at the river steps; no F on her forearm because her Federation tattoo was somewhere else.

'Down there. That black kid. What's he got hold of, then?'

The Fs looked.

'Number plate...?'

''Kin *is,* in'it!'

'*Could be,* that's all.' Queen Max stared hard. 'Keep a tag on him!' she commanded Charlie. 'Snuff an' me'll go on looking. You get its number.'

'Get him an' all?'

'Get back to me. Driving round our streets, knocking over our kids...if that car's come off the Barrier there's gonna be the biggest war since Hitler. Don't you spoil that.'

'Yeah.'

'...So nothin' *drastic,* not yet.'

'Right.'

And two Fs went up in a clenched fist salute.

Laura had split with her father. He'd do the streets, the bus stops and the park. She'd go where she'd gone with Kaninda the day before, through the Barrier Estate and along the riverside walk.

Three girls about eleven or twelve were having a smoke and a giggle on one of the benches; one sitting on the backrest, big boots, white legs crossed, flicking her ash as if she were up at the bar in Flamingos.

'Three tickets for Screen Two!' she shouted at Laura.

Predictable. And an old one – they really ought to change the look of these God's Force uniforms. But there was no Kaninda here burning his lips on a Silk Cut.

It was getting past the younger kids which was always the chancy business. A stand up and a salute; a plea to let them shake her tambourine; or a 'give us a cup o' soup' – the smaller the kid the less you knew what to expect. And a mean little knot of Barrier kids were kicking a plastic bottle to death in a game of football, girls and boys. One of the girls Laura knew – Sharon – who was ten or eleven and had been to a God's Force Friday Club party once, a little leader who could easily have been with the smokers back along the walk.

Laura got in first. 'You seen a black boy on his own?'

'We got Jackson here.'

Jackson was too young, big eyes, football feet dancing round the girls and getting fouled all the time with cuddles. He showed up at Junior God's Force when there were prizes to be had.

'Older.'

'Oh, yeah? Theo done a runner on you?'

Growing up too fast, Sharon was. 'No, as it happens. Another boy, he's in a white shirt and grey trousers. Bit younger.'

'What's it worth?'

'He's lost, that's all. No big deal. I want to find him.'

'You wanna find a lot of things.'

It stopped Laura there. 'What d'you mean by that?' The kid had a real knowing look on her face.

'You wanna find Heaven for a kick-off, don't you?'

Laura didn't think a member in uniform ought to clout a kid round the cheeky head. 'Where is he? It's important.'

'Looking at the mud. Looks like he thinks he's gonna find treasure.'

'GOAL!' The plastic bottle kicking game hadn't stopped for any of this.

'You playin' or not, Sha? Went right through your legs.'

'I'm talkin', aren't I?'

But Laura hurried on. There was only one way down to the Thames mud, unless you fell from the railings – over the locked gate and down the steps; she and Theo sat there sometimes. But that Sharon had unsettled her with her savvy little attitude; and when you were guilty as hell anyway, you could well do without savvy little attitudes...

Kaninda was no fool. Lying low till he was ready meant it was only a matter of time before he took the walk back or let himself be found. They'd think he was being good, but he was only being good the way a kraal of prisoners sit with their hands on their bowed heads. Waiting... He ran his fingers over the smooth of the number plate, angled it this way and that to see how the little cells sparkled in the sun, gave off good reflections. The plates in Lasai were a different shape; square, and made of dull tin with most numbers painted on by hand. People *made* their plates in Lasai, they didn't buy them, even if they got a new car.

And till the day someone shot him dead he would always remember the plate on their jeep: 385 KEN – all Katonga letters starting with a K, and their own plate almost saying his name. While this one in his hand had an extra letter in front, like the Yusulu government vehicles – that hated G.

And because of the G and on an impulse Kaninda threw it out into the river as far as he could manage; a grenade throw taught by the sergeants, his arm swinging upwards and letting go at the top of the arch, his wrist giving it a last professional flick.

It was a good throw. The plate splashed way out into the deeper flow of the river. Sergeant Matu would have been proud to see it. If he'd been alive.

'No keeping kids away from water, is there?'

Kaninda turned round to face up the steps. The girl Laura was coming over the gate.

'What are you doing down there?'

Kaninda turned away. Nothing was her business.

'Dad's worried about you.'

Your dad – not my dad.

'So, are you coming back, or going for a swim?'

There was an English way of saying where she could go with her questions – they said it all the time in Lasai City; it started with an 'F'. But he answered by going up the steps and climbing over the gate ahead of her, walked on through the estate.

'You're not going to run off from the school tomorrow, are you?' That was Laura.

And, 'Oi, I wanna word wi' you!'

That was someone else, someone Kaninda had spotted tracking parallel across the walkway, a Chinese. So he didn't break step, because turning round to a voice shows you've got the jumps – they'd been taught that when they went stealing in markets. He walked on and Laura ran to catch up with him, just as Lieutenant Peter came hot up the steps from the street.

'Kaninda! God be praised.'

Charlie Ty doubled back to the river, spitting and swearing, looking up and down the steps before following them at a distance and reporting back to Queen Max.

'He must've slung it in the river.'

'So you didn't see no number?'

'He done it 'fore I got there.'

'You useless—'

'But I'll know 'im again. I *clocked* 'im. 'E'll tell me the number. You don' forget them things...'

'He'd better! I want those hit an' run *punished,* 'fore they go away inside.'

'Yeah...' And even Charlie Ty smiled at the thought of that.

CHAPTER FIVE

The school was so tall it looked like an office block. In Lasai it was only offices, government buildings, the Nile Hotel and the Lulonga Road police station that went up this high – the last, they said, also going down many floors underground, deep enough for the screaming not to be heard. But the screaming coming from this London school was only kids in the yard – not Kibu men and women being asked questions by the police: *that* screaming comes up deep from the throat.

Kaninda read the name at the school entrance. 'Victoria Comprehensive School'. *Victoria, Victoria, Victoria* – there were Victorias all over Lasai City – a street, a market, a clock tower – as well as in all the school books: because the Yusulu were happy with the fat English queen whose explorers had found diamonds in their tribal lands.

He wanted to put his fingers in his ears, like before an explosion. There was a dull drone about England, a throbbing noise everywhere that had dinned into his head when he'd woken. To an ear tuned for the snap of a twig it assaulted him, bore into him. The roar of London. And the traffic was endless – cars, lorries, huge buses, going nowhere most of the time, long queues kicking out choking exhaust. Another assault on clean African lungs.

Only the no-sleep of the flight had made him tired enough not to dream the dream the night before. For one night he had not seen Gifty's torn and twisted face grinning at him, the good, soft little girl turned by death to a monster. On this Monday morning he'd woken without the run of his own sweat and fear soaking and screwing the sheets. And he felt guilty about that, too.

He walked in through the school gate with Mrs Captain Betty Rose, who would have held his hand if he'd let her. Laura came behind, had said nothing to Kaninda all morning, which was the way he wanted it – before she bolted into a gang of girls when the boy Theo started coming for them. Captain Betty had stooped to pick a stone from in her shoe, and the boy did the quickest ever face-about when he suddenly saw the woman over their heads. From waving at Laura he was suddenly reaching high at a volley ball. 'Mine!'

A few kids spoke to Captain Betty, but the rest got out of her way. Most of everybody else was attending to their own affairs, and Kaninda was taken across the yard and into the building where he was put before the school secretary, who allocated him to a class: his eyes on the floor, a prisoner's patience. The principal, a small, fast woman called Mrs Goldstein, said 'Hello' and some words of welcome, told Kaninda – with a rub of his head which he shook off fast – that the school was proud to be adding him to its United Nations. But she soon cut off Captain Betty from telling the full story of the God's Force mission to Lasai – briskly, like Kaninda's mother with the women selling cheap pens and pads outside the main post office. And before he knew it, Kaninda was sitting at a desk in a classroom, staring at his hands while a roomful of students stared at him.

It was what they called here a 'tutor group', with a young woman called Miss Mascall the teacher – who talked to the others like a student herself.

'Turn your collar down, Ruby, that's not school dress...'

'She's got a love-bite, miss.'

'Well, show it, girl, make us all jealous,' said Miss Mascall.

Not like Teacher Setzi at the Katonga High School who had a cane called Big Master hanging on the door under his hat and who dragged you out for cuts if you spoke in the room without putting up your hand.

The Katonga High School, on the same site as the Katonga Mine...

The mine was still and quiet the day after the collapse of Deep Road Nine. It always was still and quiet; on the surface there was never any sign of what went on half a mile below; but this was a special quiet, a waiting quiet, a heavy the-rains-are-coming quiet. Kaninda's father had come home with the terrible news of so many killed, and of the manager's decision to wall up the tunnel and not go digging for corpses. 'They're buried already,' he'd said, 'they only need the prayers.' Nothing was said about 'sorry' or regrets to Kibu families.

Workers' meetings were held that night in the township, blazing torches and a glow in the sky; but nothing seemed to come from it but the wailing of the women and the chanting for the passing of the spirits: no sounds of riot. All the same, Kaninda's father bolted the iron gates of their garden and left the dogs outside. And the next day the school opened as usual because nobody seemed to know what else to do. Kaninda's father went to work, but he took a rifle with him in the car in case he was attacked for being management, with the promise he'd come home to stop Kaninda and Gifty going to their schools if there was any trouble. But he didn't return, just telephoned to say that everywhere was quiet. Very quiet...

Many children were absent, and no one expected them to be there; these were the children whose fathers had been trapped and suffocated when Deep Road Nine had fallen in on them. Others said their own fathers had gone to the sacred Saconga Tree for a meeting. So lessons began, with Teacher Setzi very stiff and tense and no blinks, and no threat of Big Master needed in the room that morning. It was eyes hard down at work on a sheet of mathematics.

When in came the K Security men, the real Big Masters at the Katonga Mine; six of them, not dressed too differently to the government police, but carrying older weapons. Sounds in the corridor said they were also going into other rooms.

'Come!' one of them said to Teacher Setzi, while the others stood with their backs to the lines of students, not worried about any problem from that direction.

Teacher Setzi stood, and at the point of a gun

barrel walked out of the room. The students all stood up with him, which was the rule. And they were all still standing, not saying a word – although not for fear of Big Master – when they heard the shooting in the yard.

The shooting, and the screaming. Katonga High was a bungalow school, and the yard was a pounded earth courtyard surrounded by the classrooms. Windows were small, but now every student in the school somehow found a space for looking out – at a heap of teachers' bodies in the centre of the yard, men and women, fallen all over each other like kids in a crazy game of 'sleeping crocs'. But the worst was seeing Teacher Setzi move on the top of the heap, and the rifle go to the back of his head. Bang.

The K Security turned in their firing lines to face out, towards the classrooms. Kaninda and the rest ran like wild rabbits to hide under their desks, violence and the wind of fear stirring the room and causing Big Master to sway on the door under Teacher Setzi's hat, the room filled with panic breathing, and the sound of sicking up. Until a megaphone shouted, 'Dismiss!' in the voice of the school principal. 'School closed.' And Kaninda and the rest went fearfully out into the yard and ran round the stench of burning corpses to their homes, to hear the talk of other brains in the Kibu community being massacred around Lasai.

'Jon Bennett, you just blew it!' Miss Mascall suddenly looked up from the roll-call. 'We had a deal and you blew it! Literally.'

'What?'

'You know. I said make that noise in this room again and you don't go on the trip.'

'What noise? Wasn't me!'

'I know your smell!'

And that *did* get the students going. Hands to their noses, collars pulled up over their faces like raiders' masks. And Kaninda could smell it now, spicy food gone foul.

'Can't prove that was mine!'

'I don't have to.' Miss Mascall slapped the roll-call shut. 'I choose who I take on the factory trip; health and safety; it's a food factory.'

'Don' wanna go anyhow!'

Kaninda expected to see a Big Master come out from somewhere; but it didn't; and soon he'd got used to the noise and the talking-back in the English school. He followed the trail to French and then to Science – new books growing fat under his arms till he was given a locker – before everyone dropped out into the yard again for break. This game called obedience, holding himself normal when inside he wanted to scream his head off and throw himself into the road under those heavy wheels. But somehow he held himself in. There was more he had to do before he could rest 'not guilty' in a two-foot grave.

A jumbo jet passed low over the school, could be flying into the same airport he'd come to. And he asked himself how many more kids from Lasai might be up there in the sky. Kids without families; Kibu kids who'd lived.

Laura must have got off to sleep towards morning because when the alarm clock rang she came from somewhere else. But she had had a terrible night. The bedclothes told their story of the turmoil she was in. She'd kicked about and got her legs so entangled that she'd yanked off her pyjama bottoms and thrown them at the door. She'd tried praying – for that girl in the gutter, for forgiveness, for some peace of mind. Not God's Force loud praying but a personal begging to be shown what she should do. And still she'd stayed wide-eyed awake.

Making her bed, she looked at the one picture on her wall that wasn't religious, a magazine picture of her mother's island in the Seychelles. White sand, coconut palms reaching out over the sea, a giant tortoise, the island they reckoned was the original Garden of Eden. Paradise.

Well, that was the sort of earthly paradise she went for, far away from the grief of Thames Reach. What *had* her mother been thinking about to leave a place where there's no word in the language for 'racism', where there's no violent crime, where there's food in the sea for all and coconut milk for ever, where you could grab at life, go for it, be 'sool' as Theo put it?

So how far away was this paradise?

Now, at school break-time, Laura ran to Theo in the yard; there'd been no privacy in class for a word with him, but out here among the other hundreds they could be on their own.

'Laura, baby, you got no *shine* today!'

'So tell me what's to shine about?'

'Knowin' me, Sis. "Rodeo an' Juliet".'

'You mean "Romeo".'

'I mean "Rodeo" – get off my back!'

Was that a joke or did he mean it? Laura grabbed Theo, turned him round and pushed him into a corner. 'Talk sense sometime in your life!' she shouted at him. 'Face facts once in a while...'

'What facts do I face?'

'You *know* what facts...'

'Neg-a-tive! I got a *blur*, nothink more.' He waved a hand across his eyes. 'We was in the car, you was driving, and a kid ran out an' you swerved, and the kid weren't there no more.'

'They're hard facts, man!'

'Nah, it was all in a scoot. They ain't proof you ran over the kid an' killed it.'

'*We!*' Laura wanted to hit him. That look in his eyes, the denying, she hated him for it. She wanted a plan, she wanted a way that they could both go and tell the police they did it and get their punishment over.

'They'd kill us, the Ropeyard Fed's, if they was on the same facts as you. You c'n forget police, that'd be the easy bit, doin' time in Feltham...'

Then he smiled at her, all cocky, all washing-his-hands, and she pulled her arm back to clout him.

Anyone listening would have heard a strangled cry.

Kaninda had come into the yard where there was no one he wanted to know and no one he wanted to find. He was somehow going to get himself through to the end of the day without committing violence on himself, through to the end of the week, through till the rains came if he had to; he was going to reconnoitre the terrain and somehow work out how to get home to Lasai – to take his revenge for the death of his family. Because there would be cousins somewhere, even the Yusulu wouldn't have killed *all* the Kibu. And the Colonel, 'The Leopard', was still gathering the rebels for the big push on the government forces; it might be now, it might be after the rains; no matter, so long as Kaninda got there some time for the killing.

The school yard was crowded like the outside of Victoria Stadium for the Africa Cup. Each way you turned they were talking, eating, spitting, pushing about; girls and boys. But over at the edge, near the gate to the road, there was space where he could stand and think and hold himself together.

Except, in Kaninda's way to getting there stood that big, tall Chinese boy, and mean-looking like K Security. The tracking boy from the river front the day before.

'Oi! You!'

Kaninda ignored him, went to walk on past, but was stopped by a rough grab at his arm; at his bullet-hole arm. He looked at the face of the big Chinese, screwed up with cold power.

'Take off my arm!' Wait your chance.

'Yeah, I'll take off your arm! Right off! An' your 'ead!'

The Chinese squeezed him harder, hurt the hole

in Kaninda that had been his only body pain when his family had died; the wound he carried like a guilty medal he'd been awarded.

'That car plate you 'ad...'

'Take off!' Kaninda tried twisting, slipping out. But the Chinese dug in his nails now and hurt him more.

'What number was it, arsehole?' He put his pimply face closer.

Now Kaninda hurt badly – the arm, and the spirit: he was near to breaking.

'Eh?' Another twist.

But Kaninda was trained. A last try. 'Take off – you got me?'

'Start talkin'! That number...'

But he got no more out, other than a sweaty groan. As his lips curled with cruel contempt and his fingers dug hard into Kaninda's muscle, like a strongbow bolt Kaninda's free hand shot forward at groin level, hard and fast as if he were going right on through – and grabbed fierce on his parts, which he twisted up and sharp to the right as if he might screw things off; all one movement with a hold like the jaw lock of a fighting dog, throwing his own head back so he couldn't be butted.

'Take off my arm!'

No problem, the Chinese had already taken off;

both his hands which had shot down to Kaninda's wrist, wrestling it.

'Aaaagh!'

Which let Kaninda lunge with his released hand for the neck, a choking grip where the thumb pressed hard at the windpipe. The Chinese eyes bulging, Kaninda walked him round in a full circle, like a trainer with a colt, feeling strong, feeling detonated.

'Surrender, you?'

The Chinese was up on his toes, someone wanting to fly, one hand below, one hand at his neck. His face was twisted now not with power but with pain and choke.

'Don't touch again!' And with a last rip and dig of his nails, Kaninda screwed the Chinese away, pushed back his neck, and walked off, knowing the other would never risk an attack from behind on such a fighter.

He could have done worse to him; but soldiers fought for objectives. You captured without killing if you wanted information, you finished off if it was them or you. Or you taught a lesson if it was someone who had stolen your rations. He had controlled the urge to kill, and this Chinese had been taught a lesson. Don't ever put a hand on Kaninda's wound. And it had happened with hardly any sound, and not many people knowing.

Theo being one of them, though.

'Ken! Pos-i-tive, man! You got some guts!'

Kaninda said nothing – there was nothing to say: and he was still swallowing the spit of violence.

'He's one of the Federation. They "cut" to get in. You made the wrong enemy there!'

'No. Chinese making the wrong enemy. Chinese *got* the wrong enemy. I know all right, wrong enemies!'

'Well, I'm a good friend, mate, when you're picking sides.'

But Kaninda had no more to say. Wiping his hands down his shirt, he walked on over to the gate where he'd been heading, to find that space he wanted, to breath very, very deep.

CHAPTER SIX

It was very public, where they saw people at Thames Reach police station. No sit yourself down, private interview, cup of tea, have a fag, phone your brief; it was stand on your side of a security screen and talk through the drilled perspex holes, with the rest of the world waiting behind you to show their drivers' licences or get their bail forms signed.

'We've got the statements,' the policewoman told Rene Hedges. 'We're doing what we can till the child—' she found the name – 'till Dolly wakes up and talks to us.'

'You got "red car an' no plates"?' Rene wanted to know.

'Yup. So we can't do a trace on the computer...'

'So what else you doin'? If she dies an' don't talk to you – which she won't then, will she – is that the end of it? Shelf it – unsolved crime? Typical!'

A man behind Rene dropped his MOT.

'No, madam. It's on everyone's day sheet; it's on the Yard list. Every officer in London will be on the lookout...'

'Yeah, I can just see that!' Rene lit a cigarette and blew smoke at the 'No Smoking' sign. 'Top of their list, I bet!' She pushed her face at the perspex. 'They'll do me for loitering quick enough, but when a little girl's been run down, what action do we see then? You got the direction the red car went off in?'

The policewoman looked at the file. 'No. Has anyone said that?'

'They have.'

'It's not down here.' She flapped over the pages.

The motorist coughed and Rene Hedges looked round and perished him. 'Must've been someone talking to me.'

'This someone being an eye witness?'

Rene nodded, as if the policewoman were a child slow on the uptake – but some sharp interest was coming through the small perspex holes.

'So which direction did it take?'

'Allegedly, it turned right.'

'Right?' The policewoman skewed the map of the incident. 'Which leads to...'

'The river, the Barrier Estate.'

'Right...'

'So that's where we wanna see a bit of action. I'n it? Because if my Doll was the kid of someone with a bit of dosh we'd soon see every door knocked down, wouldn't we?' Rene turned to the MOT man for support. He dropped his licence this time. She stubbed out her fag in the metal trough for passing documents through. 'You get round the Barrier Estate an' start askin' questions there – that's what you wanna do!'

The policewoman looked down at the fag end, up at Rene Hedges. 'I'll definitely pass this on,' she said.

Kaninda and Theo were out of school, down at the walkway which runs from the Barrier Estate along to the Thames flood defence itself. Here by the riverside Kaninda was close enough to see the rivets on the plates of the Barrier's steel piers, bright in the sun and glinting.

He did not want to be here, but Theo had joked him out of the school yard, the way Sergeant Matu got people to give him cigarettes.

'Ken – wanna show you something a bit awesome...'

'"Awe-some"?'

'"Awesome's" what you're gonna see.'

And Kaninda went with him, only partly because he was being pulled, only partly because of the boy Theo being like Sergeant Matu kidding, mostly because the boy had seen him defeat the Chinese. He needed to be the calm Kaninda again, not someone special at fighting.

It was the meal break, people were allowed out of the school yard. Theo showed him how to give a meal ticket to a woman in a white hat and pick up a pack of sandwich and an apple, which they ate as they hurried along the road to the river.

'Suthink I wanna know if you reckon you can do.'

'I swim.'

'Neg-a-tive! Not in them swirls. Get sucked under like down a plug 'ole.'

Kaninda was a good swimmer. His father had taught him among the papyrus beds fringing the river where they fished, their clothes on a stunted acacia tree. But the cold of this river would be different – things floating and swirling showed it surging with currents. You only swam in such treacherous waters for reasons of life and death.

'I c'n see you got some bottle, Ken...'

Kaninda didn't understand.

'You got...guts.'

No reply. Guts was courage, wasn't it? Well, he

didn't 'have' courage, they'd shot it into him.

Theo was leaning on the wooden rail that ran along the river's edge, metres above the tide coming in. Running across the river was the Thames Barrier, and on the other bank, down-stream, the large ship was still moored up at the factory jetty Kaninda had seen before.

'It's what you got to do...'

Theo was looking at him; this was why they were here. This *awesome* thing.

'...to get into the Crew.'

'"Crew"?'

'The Barrier Crew. The lads – an' girls, some. The gang, like, the brothers an' sisters. From where we live. To get in the Crew you gotta show you got guts.'

'If you *want* this Crew...' Kaninda's closed face opened to show contempt. Kids! School yard gangs!

'Yeah, if... Wassup, don't you want be one of the brothers? You could do it, Ken. Look, see back there?' Theo pointed downstream along the walkway, where the wooden-topped railing ran. 'This straight bit, to the monkey climb...' The railing ran along to a small children's play area, then took a turn along to a jetty. 'Hundred metres and thirty-six posts.' He smacked the wooden railing, which was about thirty centimetres wide and slightly ridged. Blue metal posts topped by squat round caps came every two-and-a-half metres. 'You run along the top of this to the monkey climb down there.'

Kaninda's face had gone back to showing no expression, his eyes slits in the brightness off the water.

'Any poof could walk it, slow. To get in the Crew you run along like in the Olympics, only stepping over all the posts, an' do it in under thirty seconds...'

Kaninda looked along and back.

'Or you don't. You're too slow or you fall off. Which ain't serious this side of the rail, but that...'

Theo pecked a finger over at the water of the Thames, lapping up the river wall beneath them.

'You are wet.'

'No, son, you are killed. 'Cos you 'ave to do it at low tide, when all you got down there is rocks an' stones.'

Kaninda looked again along the rail, pictured it: bare feet, arms out for balance, the river arm up to tip him inwards if he slipped.

'*Thirty* seconds?'

Theo nodded, serious stuff. 'Told you, "awesome".'

Kaninda stared him in the face. 'Give time for

eating my apple and go back!' All the platoon in their real war could have done this.

Theo's yoop made a seabird take off. 'Pos-it-ive! You're my man, Ken!' He slapped Kaninda a hard one on the back. 'You're good as Crew – gotta be our man, the way you saw off Charlie Ty!'

But Kaninda wasn't slapping back, wasn't shaking Theo's hand. He was turning away and looking out over the water.

'I got my clan,' he said. 'I don't want clan from you.'

Colonel Munyankindi couldn't afford to feed anyone who couldn't fight. Street kids, orphans, refugees running from the terror of Lasai – 'the Leopard' wasn't giving out Red Cross aid, he was leading the Kibu fight against the Yusulu. He couldn't take on anyone who wasn't going to be a top grade fighter. But age didn't come into it. If you were strong enough to carry an M16 and three belts of bullets round your neck, if you had a dead eye for a target, if you didn't limp disabled or run with dysentery you could be put up for a recruit. If you could kill.

Which was the test – set up in a clearing with a Yusulu prisoner tied to a post with a sack over his head. You were given the gun, and you had to shoot him dead – fast. From the second you saw him and were given the order you were timed; and if you waited more than five seconds you were useless. Such kids were beaten, thrown out or abused. Sergeant Matu said it all the time, 'One second wait and fifteen rounds is coming at you, you got me? Fighting, you got no time for a talk with your nerves.'

The early weeks after the massacre of his family Kaninda had been with the Lasai street kids, he hadn't followed the pathetic Kibu families on their trek. When they got across the border they'd just as likely be killed by some other clan. But there had always been the truants, the run aways, the orphans, the outcasts of Lasai city life. Street kids were what these people became, unless they were willing to go to a Mission and give their lives to the Lord Jesus. And Kaninda vowed his life was going to be given to one thing only – revenge for the deaths of his mother, his father and little Gifty. Being an outlaw was the only thing he could *be. So he tagged on and ran the streets with them – one arm hanging till the flesh wound started to heal, till the exercise he gave the muscle began to bring back some of its strength. Till he could steal food, jump Yusulu businessmen for their spectacles, dip into cars which didn't carry the government G; one of a loose band of tough kids who were rarely the same gang two days together – someone arrested, someone sick and dying, someone shot for looting.*

It was a Kibu raid on the post office that gave him a run in the right direction. The Yusulu government was putting in new cables to its telecommunications system, with trenches dug along the Lebonga Road from the post office to the transmitter masts on the hill. New trenches were dug every day which the rats took time to discover and were cleaner places to sleep than rubbish skips and rain drains.

One night without moon a platoon of the Kibu rebel army hit the post office with hand grenades tied into slings. They crept along the main trench flushing out the street kids like rats themselves; but Kaninda had got himself inside a length of drainage pipe, and had no time to move.

He lay there with his breath held and his body tense as the rebel platoon stood up on the command and swung their sacked grenades.

'Stand. Pin out! *Hold – one, two. Go!'*

The soldiers slung their grenades underarm and accurate, nine out of ten in through the target windows. Throwing themselves flat in the trench, they covered their heads as glass flew, earth spat, eardrums were blasted and the ground shook. On the order the men ran crouching along the length of the trench to the truck waiting with its engine revving.

Only as it swayed away at speed towards the bush did the sergeant count his men and find he had one over.

'Who are you?'

'Kibu.'

'Name?'

'Kaninda Bulumba.' Not easy to say with a boot across his neck. But he could wave his rough healed arm at the man. 'Everyone killed by Yusulu...'

'You not killed too?' The hard sole came off his windpipe.

'If I was, you're talking to a ghost!'

The truck was speeding and bumping, the bush and its cover was near, the post office back in Lasai was burning orange and black in the sky. So it might have been the elation at a successful raid that made Sergeant Matu laugh at this cheeky boy. Or he might have seen the fire in Kaninda's eyes.

'Why are you in this truck?'

Kaninda was being allowed to get up. 'I'm going to be a Kibu soldier. I'm going to kill Yusulu.' Not I want to *but* I'm going to.

Now he had his chance to do it. He was ten

metres from the prisoner tied to the post.

'This man has raped, burned and shot Kibu people,' Sergeant Matu snapped.

Kaninda saw his father and mother in their hot, blood-wet heap on the floor, he saw Gifty where her little body had slid down the wall. He smelt the burning flesh of the Kibu teachers at his school. His mouth filled with saliva which tasted of blood. 'Weapon!' snapped Sergeant Matu. The M16 was put in Kaninda's arms. It was heavy, like his father's typewriter. 'I give the order and you shoot!'

Kaninda ducked his head.

'Fire!'

And within the count of three Kaninda lifted the weapon, took aim, and squeezed at the trigger. The M16 kicked, the sound stunned, the barrel pushed up and to the right, the heel wrenched at his weakened muscle – but by the way the Yusulu jerked at the post the first rounds must have hit him. Kaninda kept his finger squeezed; they had to take the weapon off him – as the prisoner stood up straight and took the sack off his head himself, hadn't been tied at all. The rounds had been blanks. Like the living dead he walked towards Kaninda.

'Good,' he said. 'You eat.'

And that was the initiation. Kaninda was a rebel soldier.

It was as if Theo never heard the word 'no', as if his brain didn't recognise it. He was still all arms round Kaninda, walking him away from the Barrier along past the children's playground – its squared ropes and swinging knot-ends like a small Kibu training ground – and through to the estate where Laura had first taken him to the river.

'C'mon. We got time for a wet.'

Kaninda went along with him. A 'wet' wouldn't be a swim but it could be a drink or a pee, both OK.

They swung round a wall painted all over with words and designs, to be faced suddenly by a policeman.

'Hello, lads.'

'Wotcha!' But Theo wasn't going to stop.

'Oi!' The policeman grabbed him by the shoulder. 'I want a word.'

Theo clutched at his shoulder, winced like someone easily bruised. 'A word? That's handy – I know a million o' them. Give us a favourite letter an' I'll pick you one...'

Kaninda shut his eyes. This was like at the school. In Lasai City – even before the rebels – Theo would have been rifle butted to the ground for such cheek.

'A word?' The policeman let go. 'Here's one. "Red". "Red car".'

'Cheating, man! That's two. An' you're picking 'em for me.'

'No, I'm asking them, lad.' The policeman was older than Kaninda's father, back in Lasai he would have been behind a big bare desk, not patrolling out in the city. 'Have you seen a red car—?'

'Streetfuls of 'em!'

'Without plates?'

Theo thought for a moment and shook his head as if something so illegal was the last thing he'd see.

Kaninda stood and watched, his eyes tighter slits than on a hillside look-out. Theo *had* seen such a car; Kaninda had seen such a car; Theo's brother was the owner of such a car, and Kaninda had thrown such a number plate out into the mud. So?

The policeman turned to look at Kaninda. 'What about you?'

Interrogation. Look down, give nothing at first, harden your belly because that's where the kicks come when they want you to talk – if they were going to kill you from the first you wouldn't still be standing there. Then weaken. Say something false but believable, but never know the detail, just always have something you've got to show them: you need to see the building, or recognise the tree, or walk the path till you come to what will jog your memory for them – all chances to make a run. Lead them on as long as you can, because they're going to kill you anyway...

'He only—' Theo started.

'*He'll* tell me!' The policeman stared down at Kaninda, but Kaninda sensed that Theo had the sharper need to know what he was going to say.

'New. From Lasai, just,' Kaninda said, shaking his head. What could such a newcomer with poor English know about this place and its colours of cars...?

The policeman looked ready to move on when a hot voice came round the corner.

'I ain't got all day, I'm at work one o'clock.'

It was the woman Lydia, coming from the flats in front of another policeman, younger. She saw Theo.

'Theo – ain't you in school?'

Theo searched himself. 'No, feels like I'm here. It's dinner break.'

'Don' be late. I don' want no late marks on your profile!' She suddenly turned on the policeman who'd come with her. 'You got a search warrant?'

'A search warrant?'

'I jus' thought – if you wanna search somewhere you got to have a search warrant, i'n that right?' She was standing with her head doing a little shake like a small engine running.

'Only for official searches.'

'So this ain't official? Well, then—'

'Look, miss, you're helping us.' This was the older policeman. 'Local residents say you've got a red car...'

The younger one chipped in. 'You admit to having a red car.'

'Admit?! Like it's some crime?'

'No, love. That's the point. You've got a red car, you give us a look at it, we go away, you're eliminated from enquiries...'

Theo started singing. 'E-limin-ation, it's the name of the game...'

'Or we get a search warrant, come back, and waste twice your time and all that public money.'

Lydia frowned. 'So, *what* is it you're looking for ex-act?'

'We'll know. You just show us, eh? There's a good—'

But Lydia was moving off towards the lock-ups taking out a leather pouch of keys.

It came to Kaninda suddenly that this Lydia didn't know what they were looking for. He and Theo did, from the talk of the older policeman; but she didn't. They wanted to find a red car with no number plates, and she only knew red car. Yet on

Saturday she'd locked up such a car...

Kaninda looked at Theo, and knew the two of them were having the same thoughts. She was going to open the door on what these police were looking for.

'Hey, Lyd!' Theo shouted.

'What?' She let it stop her, key in the lock.

'That's Mal's place, hon. Mal pays the rent, he's gotta give the word...'

Lydia stared at Theo, pondered on this.

'Come on, Miss.' And the older policeman twisted the key in the lock and lifted the up-and-over door.

Kaninda heard Theo groan, just a soft groan, something for inside himself.

Up went the metal door, down went the eyes to where there wouldn't be any plates – to see the red car tucked away neatly, with a dirty rear plate legally in place, looking rusted on.

The policeman checked with his notebook. 'Malcolm Julien, registered owner. Thank you, Miss. See – that's all we're doing.'

'Only your job, i'n it?' Theo said.

But Kaninda sensed he could have danced and sung it; there was a bounce in his step going back to the school that was left foot festival, right foot celebration. He skipped it round Kaninda, enthused.

'Good fighter, smart talker – you're a Barrier brother you are, Ken...'

'No,' Kaninda told him, staying out of step. 'Kibu soldier. Captured Kibu soldier...'

CHAPTER SEVEN

The food was different, and anger makes it hard to digest – so Kaninda was getting pain in the top of his chest, with the taste of sick coming back at him. His family used to sit up at the table together and dip into dishes of plantain, beans and peas, rice, long sweet potatoes, groundnuts, cassava, sometimes fish, sometimes meat – always a meal Kaninda's mother had taken time cooking. 'I don't work at the food for you to look at,' she'd tell Gifty who ate like a sunbird. And they would talk. Food was more than food, it was them all together. But here in London Mrs Captain Betty Rose pulled packets out of the freezer, pushed them into a microwave and served them to him and the girl sitting up in the kitchen like two people at a matoke café counter: chicken bits in watery curry, and chips, with beans from a tin. To drink there was water from the tap.

In Lasai water had a bitter taste, and nobody who could afford otherwise drank it. Kaninda's father drank beer, and the rest had Seven-Up: that was when Kaninda was a kid, before river water was his soldier's boil-up.

'Con-venience!' Captain Betty told Kaninda, clattering down a cold plate. 'Saturday I'll cook you Seychelles sailfish and coconut curry, but this week God's made me *busy*. Praise indeed!'

Kaninda ate the food like doing a task; because his arms needed building, his legs had to have strength, his muscles needed to get hard. If you left food in the Kibu camp Sergeant Matu cuffed you for it. *'Your lackin' of strength could be paid up in my blood, you got me?'* He was always right; and now Kaninda needed all his strength to get back to Lasai; to swim it if he had to.

'See how you like it!' Captain Betty said, pulling off her apron.

Kaninda looked at his empty plate. He'd eaten it, without letting it taste. He looked at the wall, his inside pushing down on a hot stab of wind.

'We c'n fix you up with clothin' later...'

She was talking about where they were going, all of them; the girl Laura – wearing church uniform like the woman – and the man. To Junior God's Force. Kaninda swore inside his head. He hated the church, everything connected with it. Part of the driving him out the day before had been the voices, the high harmonising women's voices like hearing his mother and the Sisterhood at the Apostles' Chapel – her voice reaching up to the top notes, nearly as high as she had screamed. As his father had screamed... But he knew about obedience; if he ran off to the river at every God's Force meeting they'd start locking him in his room. He'd swallow his bile and obey until his time came.

'Dishwasher!' Captain Betty said. 'A gift an' all to busy people, thank the Lord.'

Kaninda obeyed, stacked his plate and cutlery in the machine.

'Now brush your teeth.'

He obeyed again, a give-no-trouble captive. He knew behind his back Mrs Captain Betty Rose was shaking her head at the girl – at this ungrateful boy they'd brought out from Africa. He went up to the bathroom. He had no one to shake *his* head at any more, no one in the world to wink at, or pull a funny face. His mask had been welded on: a Kibu soldier's, hard and strong.

Never mind Kaninda, Laura was obeying every flick of her mother's eye. In her state of stress she kept finding the air from her lungs sucked up in sudden heaves, a surprise catching of her breath which had to be the guilt rising inside her. It caught her at awkward moments, when she had to try not to make any gasps to give herself away. In her life on every side now she was being good, God's sort of good. Secret sexy underwear was out. So were rebel dreams of swimming raw in a Seychelles sea, running up its white beach to a waiting boy like Theo, climbing curving trees for coconuts, catching land crabs, plaiting her hair with orchids – and lying on the sand and being kissed: all those rebel thoughts of paradise were blanked from her mind as soon as they came into it. Awful, sleepless nights alone with God and her guilt were telling her they were all so much wickedness, evil. Life was back to smart uniform, duty, fearing God and praising Him, asking Him for forgiveness for the terrible thing they'd done. Freedom was finished, being a God's Force little soldier again was the new beginning in her life – all in the turn-round of a day, all in the spurt of a car.

There were the regulars and the casuals at Junior God's Force. The regulars had their red and gold sweat-shirts with the GF banner embroidered on; they had their badges down their arms showing where they were in the ranks – bronze, silver, gold sword – Junior Soldiers on the march towards the badge Laura wore, the platinum Shield of Faith. The musicians among them – even the shakers and rattlers – had a golden harp on the other arm.

Then there were the casuals, like little Jackson. These were the kids who wanted in on something but weren't sure about wanting in on it week in, week out; the non-joiners who weren't looking to be members of any group or gang where you had to make a promise to God – or eat a worm or wee from a balcony – to join. Some of them were kids who went for the warm hall in the winter and the beanos in the summer, the drifters in and out who Captain Betty would never exclude while there was a chance she might bring them into the Lord Jesus's club.

But although Captain Betty and other adults were there, Junior God's Force was Laura's section, and tonight she'd prepared the activities better and with more heart than ever. All to save her soul. Tonight, after a powerful prayer, she'd got a treasure hunt set up, with clues of jumbled letters leading from one location to the next. Each team had to write their unjumbled words on clipboard sheets before they went on, there were no short cuts, no following the fastest, no cheating. The prize for the first team all correct – and they all started from different points, just the last three clues running in the same order – was a paperback gospel each.

Kaninda stood at the side of the assembly room, not joining in. The girl ignored him, throwing herself into helping each team, and once the scurry and the shouting started, he walked away, out to the back of the building where the man Lieutenant Peter was glueing a rickety chair together.

'Kaninda, could you hold this?'

Without a word or even a look at the man, Kaninda held the chair back straight while the glue nozzle was squeezed; and, he held the other chairs which needed glueing, all the while without speaking,

For twenty minutes Laura lost herself in God's Force activity, the way things had used to be before she took the rebel route. What a fool she'd been! And what punishment God had dumped upon her – putting the life of a little girl in the scales! But perhaps while she was doing God's work, He was making the little girl better, and better. Even on the off-chance, she was giving her heart to the treasure hunt, showing God's patience to a frustrated little Jackson who wasn't winning.

'Never say die, Jackson, you might win the next game...'

'Won't be here for the next game!'

Everything going on as normal – till halfway through, when Sharon suddenly showed up. No membership, a challenging face round the door, just the sort to get a pull from Captain Betty.

'Come in an' all. You want to join in the fun?'

Sharon looked at children scampering round the hall. *'Fun?'*

'Treasure hunt, an' prizes.'

Sharon was a casual among casuals, usually ended up upsetting people and spoiling what was planned. Laura could do without Sharon, any time. But the girl came further in and leaned where Kaninda had leaned, watched the unjumbling of clues with a sneer. She shouted out one of the answers, spoiling. 'O.D.O.R. *Door,* in'it! Can see that from here.' Some of the others slackened off their enthusiasm a bit because Sharon's say-so mattered; and Laura knew she'd got to get her properly involved, or get her out.

'You want to join one of the teams?'

Sharon shrugged.

'It's not too late. And there's prizes.'

'She said. Which one's winning, then?'

'Can't tell you that.'

Another shrug. Laura hovered.

'How far d'you go?' Sharon asked.

'There's ten clues...'

'No, Sat'day. In the car.'

Sharon had unjumbled Laura in one go. A wave of sickly scare rolled inside her and twisted her stomach. Her uniform collar went tight.

'What car?'

'Thought you was s'posed to tell the truth in these places.' Sharon looked round, fixed her eyes on a picture of the Lord Jesus.

'*Banner*. Is this right?'

Laura checked an answer from one of the groups. She nodded.

'He said it was *banana*. Prat!'

'There's no bananas in here.' Laura's voice was thin and absent.

'You was in Mal's car. Wi' Theo.'

'Oh! Yeah, we sat in it.'

'So?' Sharon's face had all the knowing of a pavement girl outside the Royal Artillery barracks.

'So, what?'

'How far d'you go? Let him kiss you? Feel you up?'

'Ssssh!' But Laura laughed, dry, a cackle: a laugh that stood for a big sigh of relief. That was it! Sharon wasn't on about *distance*, going for the drive; she was on about kissing and groping. Laura was certain there'd been no kids about to see them when Theo had taken off. He'd made sure.

She bought herself out of the mucky conversation. 'That group there. Claudette's. They're winning.'

So Sharon joined them, and won herself a St John's gospel.

Back in the Katonga High School Teacher Setzi had taught lessons, done nothing else. Unlike the poor government schools in Lasai, the mine school had books and desks and space for the teacher to move around the classroom. But he didn't. He sat at the front or he stood at the blackboard and he *taught*. Kaninda and the others sat in their places and they learned: or else Big Master came to help them! Teacher Setzi was their teacher, they were his students, but if they didn't learn, it wasn't his fault, it was theirs. Here in London, though, Miss Mascall did everything *except* teach. She gave out letters for something she called 'the trip', she stopped fights, shouted in people's faces, called for the deputy headmaster, told girls to pull their socks up out of their shoes so they would show, and sent boys to the lavatory to tuck in their shirts properly. Miss Mascall in the Tutor Group was involved with everything except teaching.

On the timetable she was also History and Geography. Today, Tuesday, was the first such lesson, Geography. Kaninda had dreamt his Gifty nightmare again, but this time her body had come floating down that river at him in the swirlings of the boy Theo's Barrier edge; the old Gifty, the beautiful un-shot Gifty; but she had been sucked under at the last, and at a tap on his shoulder that he'd thought was Theo, Kaninda had turned – to see her monster face pressed close to his.

He had lain there terrified. Now, this morning, under the guilty weight of still being alive, Kaninda could at least lessen it by getting his hands on a book of maps in the Geography lesson: do some planning. But all the teacher talked about was 'the trip' and gave him a letter about it, and asked him to make sure his foster mother read it. *His foster mother*! He didn't know how he stopped himself from turning the teacher's table over on top of her.

At the end she kept him behind, told him to come and stand by her. She was a big young woman, much younger than Mrs Captain Betty Rose, with red spiky hair. She looked up at him, standing with his hands clasped behind his back, the way he stood for Teacher Setzi.

'Everything OK, Kaninda?'

He knew 'OK'. Most things in Katonga and Lasai were either 'OK' or 'bad OK'. Kibu were 'OK'; Yusulu were 'bad OK'. The Kibu camp was 'OK', and London was 'bad OK' in this big way.

He stared back.

'Well, I think I'm going to make things even more OK for you...'

He sucked in breath, but only a sigh going inwards. What stupid talk was this? Was she going to put him on an aeroplane and send him home to fight the war in Lasai? That was the only 'OK' there could be in his life.

'You're our first person from Lasai, you know that? I'm really pleased to have you in my tutor group, you'll teach me a lot.' She was feeling into her handbag, but not for any aeroplane ticket, only for a comb to scratch her head. 'But another Lasain boy started today. Now—' she fixed him with pinning eyes – 'he's Yusulu, not Kibu…'

Already, Kaninda felt a killing heat boiling up inside.

'…He could be a comfort, coming from Lasai, if you want to start a new life here in London; the new generation doing better than their fathers. Or…'

Kaninda's eyes went to sniper slits.

'But he's here in the school, enrolled, so we're going to meet him.'

From the boiling Kaninda had gone fighting cold: his blood drained inward, his skin pimpled, his groin tight. He followed Miss Mascall as she led him out of the classroom and down the wide stone stairs.

'Brought out by a Red Cross mission,' Miss Mascall said. They turned the corner to the office corridor, which was empty except for a boy sitting outside the Year Head's room not looking at anything. African by colouring; London school by dress.

'Here.' Miss Mascall looked at each of them; and said firmly, 'Now you're both here for a fresh start…'

Kaninda stared at the boy, the boy stared at him. They were not the same height; Kaninda was taller.

'This is Kaninda Bulumba. And this is Faustin N'gensi.'

The boy had just the split second to lift his face to Kaninda's before he was thrown back over the low chair by the sudden crack of Kaninda's frenzied attack, a fierce chop with the hard edge of the hand to his throat and a lunge at the windpipe with guerrilla fingers.

'*Kill Yusulu*!' Kaninda shouted, backing his head for a butt to the nose before he broke the neck. '*Kill Yusulu*!'

But Miss Mascall was on him, shouting, trying to pull him off, and before he could kill Faustin N'gensi, Kaninda was hauled off and held in a fierce lock by a big tank of a teacher.

'Oi! What's he done to you?'

Others came running, and for all his training in hand-to-hand, Kaninda couldn't break free from so many of them. He went rigid, still, saved himself for the next chance. Faustin N'gensi, being helped up, mouthed a plea for protection from this mad boy.

'He's Kibu! I'm Yusulu.'

'So? You're all Thames Reach Comprehensive while you're here, sonny.' The big London teacher who was holding Kaninda in a painful lock gave him a jerk to emphasise the fact. Like Sergeant Matu with a prisoner.

Miss Mascall was pulling her jacket straight. 'Kibu and Yusulu!' she said. 'Our luck! Warring tribes.'

'As if we haven't got enough of that round here!' said the man. 'Don't know who should be seeking asylum – them or me!' He twisted Kaninda's head to face him. 'So you leave your war in Africa! Right?'

And Kaninda spat.

'So what's goin' down, man?'

'What, man?'

'You know, sho' 'nuff, don' give me no snow job. You're looking guilty as a boy comin' out of the bathroom.'

'Dunno what you're on about, brother. I'm clean, man.'

Mal had got Theo where Theo could only twist and turn, couldn't walk away – in the tight corridor of the flat between the bedrooms. He was carrying a plastic sack of new phones he'd been sent out to get, for plugging in at work. 'I'm talkin' about them plates I had to replace on the quick.'

'I never touched your plates, honest, man!'

'The car, then. Why was that engine burning hot after I'd had me dinner? An' what's this about the Babylon comin' asking Lyd to show 'em in our lock-up?'

Theo shrugged. 'They're turnin' everyone over, puttin' 'emselves about, looking busy. It's what they do, man...'

'Someone went off joyin' in that car, stone ginger certain.'

'Well, it weren't me. I was wi' Laura, 'f you remember, an' she's God's Force religious – she'd never do a bad thing like that...'

'It was someone!'

'Could be Baz Rosso, he's into a quick nick if he's gotta be somewhere fast...'

Mal thought about it. Baz Rosso ran the youth on the estate. 'Could be. Well, you hear an' I want to know...'

'Pos-it-ive, man.'

'An' I still got me eye on you. When you say "man" every other word, I'm always sussy.'

Now Theo edged round him, got in through his bedroom door – and turned the key in the lock. 'I'm clean, man, clean!' he said through the hardboard.

CHAPTER EIGHT

Kaninda Bulumba rocked on the bed, eyes tight closed, hands hard clenched – sobbing and growling like one of the victim Kibu boys going mad, the ones they drugged into being quiet. In the flashing of his screwed eyes all he could see was the stare of that Yusulu enemy come to London: N'gensi: the boy with the face of the hated tribe which had cut through his family with their bullets.

He didn't need Sergeant Matu to give the order; he had obeyed it once and been pulled off. In the longer future he went on waiting: but in the short future – tomorrow, the day after – there was no question.

Kaninda shot rigid. 'I kill him! You got me?!' he shouted at the wall.

Sergeant Matu came back to the platoon with the

news. Ambush! The colonel had reports of a convoy of Yusulu arms coming in from Uganda – good reports – and their platoon was to be the security unit.

'Assault unit does the attack but us, the security unit, does the back-up. We cover the ground going in and coming out, guide, show the quick exit route to our boats, mop up their chasers. That's us!' Sergeant Matu thumped his chest. 'Two minutes – "shoot fast, shoot last, shoot to kill"' – he shot an imaginary arc of fire from his hip.

At the first sound of 'ambush' Kaninda's blood had started to run fast – this was something for real, something to do in the war besides training.

'Ambush.' Sergeant Matu was going on, the platoon on its haunches or leaning against tree trunks or lying crossed ankles on the dry grass, nodding yeah, yeah. He was as much a teacher as Teacher Setzi, had trained himself with the best in some other war. 'Kibu choose the killing zone, but never the first place everyone thinks – because Yusulu are thinking those same thoughts...' He tapped his head wisely, and nodded. 'But we hit where there's a grade in the road, or a bend, where it slows them. We shoot up the first truck and the last, trap the rest between – and mop them up fast. Surprise! So, no talking,

no radios, no smoking, no farting.'

Someone let one off to make his point. Yeah.

'Signals are tug-wires, well hid – and the first the Yusulu know is the first big bang that hits – no whistles, no shouts to give 'em a blink to think...'

'But we're back there...'

Sergeant Matu dashed that to the ground straight off. 'We're the last away. We wave the assault men through and we stay to fight survivors.'

A rash of fear prickled over Kaninda's skin. His fingers pulled at an imaginary trigger, his left eye closed along the M16 sights. He was in the rebel army for real now, hours away from taking revenge for his mother and his father and little Gifty.

Hate killed boredom every time. If Snuff or Charlie Ty didn't feel up to raiding a shop in Millennium Mall, and if Queen Max didn't fancy selling a feel to a sad case in Ropeyard Road – so there wasn't any cash for the arcades or for 'ash' or 'rocks' or vodka – then it was pee through letterboxes, tag the F on a different wall, put in a few windows, burn out a car; do any sort of vandal stuff to pass the time. But have a hate on the boil and there was a high-priority purpose to tooling up and going somewhere – boredom gone right out of the window.

Little Dolly Hedges was the reason, Kaninda Bulumba was the target – someone from the Barrier patch who was going to be taught a lesson – and tonight was as good a night as any.

They kept it small scale. There were times for the 'all-off' – major rucks with every member of the F called up to be there – and times for private war. Tonight was grudge, for Charlie Ty's cut-down in the school yard, and so was best left to Queen Max, Snuff and Charlie himself.

'We stake-out the Barrier, get the black bastard on 'is own an' give 'im what's coming...'

'When they lug him into Casualty he won't be so lucky!'

But Kaninda didn't live on the Barrier, and tonight he was on his bed, waging his own war in his head. Coming in from three different directions, Queen Max, Charlie Ty and Snuff Bowditch met up at the river steps without a sniff of the kid they were after. Without a sniff of any kid – the walkways and squares were kid-free zones that night; there had to be something on the telly.

''E's scared to come out.'

'Messing 'is-self.'

Three tight mouths twisted on the sour breath of

gut frustration. Queen Max folded her arms, the others punched their own palms.

But not in secret. They were seen. They'd been under observation from the moment they'd headed towards each other and Snuff had spat at a Crew tag on a wall.

Baz Rosso had a top flat on the Barrier, and no one fouled in *his* lift. His mother's name was on the rent book – his Italian father long gone, cutting celebrity hair in Soho – but Baz Rosso was king of the flat, of the landing, the block, the estate. 'Barry Rosso' had at one time and another been listed on the rolls of three local comprehensives, but scrubbed off from each, and the local police files showed 'Barry Antony Arthur Rosso' as having spent time in Feltham Young Offenders' unit for violent behaviour. So he was known, and he was noted. People could do the Crew initiation a hundred times but it was Baz who gave the nod to membership. And if anyone ever wanted something to sniff, smoke or pop it was Baz Rosso they showed their money to before they went anywhere else.

His dark eyes screwed themselves, looking at the alien three down by the river steps.

'What's that, Barry? Someone at the cars?' Mrs Rosso focused on every purse of Barry's lips.

He didn't reply but shifted to get a better look,

his mouth pulled in a sneer.

'You're too good, Barry, keeping an eye for everyone...'

'Shut up!'

She did.

'That slag from the Ropeyard...' In one of his three schools Baz had forced from Maxine Bendix what the others had to give their dinner money for. He kept watching; he had eyes which didn't blink until he told them to; but he was too far up to hear what was being said down there.

'Gotta leave word!' Snuff was staring at the Crew tag on the wall, rubbing at it with the sole of a boot. 'Not come 'ere for me 'ealth.'

Charlie Ty went with him. 'Ain't goin' without some result. Blanking me on that car plate, getting lucky in the yard, little black—'

But Queen Max shut them up; she'd seen something else. Young Jackson rapping along with kicks to the rhythm at a dead plastic bottle. And wrapped up in himself, Jackson saw the three too late to go the long way round: two big whites, one big Chinese: small black boys on their own took care. He tried to turn about, swivel on a swear word, but there was one in front, one behind, one at the side – and the fourth way was a wall.

'What's your rush, Eddie Murphy?'

'Get out the way!' Jackson was nippy. He could weave a basketball between any big kid's legs, so he went for it. But he was up against a hit team. Queen Max had him like a nutcracker has a walnut. And straight off Snuff was putting in the boot.

'You got a big brother?'

'Aaaah! Get off!'

'You tell 'im this...an' this...an' this from us. We want the number off that car plate—'

'Or the missin' plate put in our 'ands—'

'Aaaah!'

'An' some respect. The Federation wants respect. Right?'

'Aaaah...!

'You tell 'im. *Right*?'

But there was nothing from Jackson. Right now all he could pass on was blood and spit, his small limbs twitching about on the fancy pattern of the council walkway.

Charlie Ty smiled, Snuff Harris stared, Queen Max with her hands on her hips was breathing deep and thrusting out with the thrill.

By the time Baz Rosso got there they'd gone, strutting off the Barrier ground like conquerors.

Jackson started to move; an eye open for any more kicks to come; a gob; and a drawing up of his legs.

'Jackson? You still got legs? Uh?'

Jackson tried them, nodded.

'I know these people. Live down the Ropeyard...'

'I never done *nothing*...'

'No? Well, I tell you, a lot gets done from now...' And Baz Rosso nodded, as if he were Al Pacino. He helped Jackson up, found the dry end of an old tissue and gave him a wipe; while like a footballer after a foul Jackson went on testing himself for serious injury as he started hobbling home.

'Jackson! This your tooth?'

Jackson ran his tongue round his mouth, spat blood again. 'Yeah,' he said. 'You c'n have it. Stick it under your pillow.'

Baz Rosso threw it at him, watched him go, then went off to find the man who knew most things among the kids, Mr Information – Theo Julien.

Theo was in the flat on his own, watching a game show. When he answered the door, Baz Rosso came right in; he always did, being someone who never stood out on anyone's front step.

'So, who *you* hiding from?'

'Me, man? No one.' Theo looked offended.

Baz waved an arm at the television. 'So this rubbish is your scene?'

'Wasn't watching, couldn't be arsed to turn it off.' But a half-drunk Coke and a dent in the cushion said otherwise. 'I'm waiting for somethink.' He pulled his Theo-the-jester face. '"*Gardenin' World.*" How to grow stuff, know what I mean? So what you want, well as the end of my Coke?'

Baz wiped his mouth with a finger and a thumb. 'I wanna know what's occurring. Uh? Maxine Bendix and a Chinese kid just give a big kicking to little Jackson.'

'Charlie Ty?'

'He hang around wi' Maxine?'

Theo nodded.

'So you tell me what they want up here.'

Theo thought about it, very fast.

'Could be Ken. This African kid...' He told Baz the tale of Kaninda in the school yard, how he'd handled himself cool and made Charlie Ty look like Noddy. 'He's prime Crew, I tell you. Sool.' But he said nothing about any joy ride in Mal's car and a little girl run over down in Ropeyard Road, where those others had come from.

'So this Ken has to be good – if he's starting the war. Uh?'

'The *war*?'

'No one hurts little kids on my patch. Not, an' gets away with it. I got a reputation...'

Theo nodded; you had to. 'You're right, Baz. Dead right.'

'So, I want to see this Ken. He starts something,

he helps the finish of it, don't he?'

'Yeah.'

'An' – you put a tape in there for me, will you? *"Gardenin' Poxy World"* – killing slugs an' creepy-creepies, I'm into all that...'

Theo smiled. Only smiled, as he picked up his flat Coke and finished it. Because he might pretend, but the fizz had gone out of him these days, def-in-ite.

It takes a long time to get to sleep when your eyes are wide with hate. Shouting at the wall hadn't been enough to give him rest. Tonight there was this new twist to Kaninda's sheets, with Faustin N'gensi's stare coming at him next to Gifty's tortured face. The pillow was soaked with the spit of anticipation before Kaninda finally slipped under into dreams. And not all war – sometime before morning his father was there as real as life, his smile, his voice, his hair lotion, the crackle of his white shirt – although in the depth of this happy time Kaninda knew that he was dead. He asked him, and the man said 'yes'.

He woke with it still fresh in his head, but straight off shouted 'Yusulu!' into his pillow. And what he carried through a Mrs Captain Betty Rose breakfast was not his father's kind face but the hateful eyes of this Faustin N'gensi. It was a sunny day as he walked to school with the silent girl Laura and he kept his head down; Sergeant Matu trained, he wouldn't look into bright light, which could ruin night vision for a month. It might be dark when he killed the Yusulu.

He knew he was ready for it when he saw the boy again. The cold skin of action raced over him but there was a school yard between the two, and a duty teacher who must have been alerted to guard the boy, so Kaninda had to turn away, spit out a full mouth of bile. Anyway, hate should never pull the trigger, the brain does that. But the target was marked. The ambush and the killing would come when its success could be as certain as a slit throat.

And two others in the yard came to him first. The Chinese boy walked past with a sweet twist on his face like someone sucking at honey. *Flag-wagging,* Sergeant Matu called it, false bravery, what they all had to show to the other side. But Kaninda knew the boy would never attack again without help – and this Kibu could slaughter an army right now.

Theo came too. Laura said something to him and he shrugged, but he didn't break step in coming to Kaninda.

'Got a message for you, Ken.'

'Don't want.'

Theo did the twist of a dance step and came back.

'Baz Rosso wants to see you.'

The slits of Kaninda's eyes asked who Baz Rosso was – if he cared.

'He's only king of the Crew. Big man. Wants a word.'

'For what, he wants?'

You could search Theo. 'For various. A little brother got kicked in last night, by your Chinese mate and his gang...'

Now Kaninda understood that tasting honey look. 'Not me doing that.'

Theo flicked his hands, cracked his fingers like whips. 'You don' have to do nothin' to get involved, man. Things happen. One thing, then somethink else. Then—'

Kaninda's mouth barely opened. 'Told you – got my clan. You got me?' The Yusulu was across the yard. He'd got the enemy clan in his sights, too, and his heart was beating fast again like at the first ambush. Any killing would be for Kibu, not this Theo.

'Then that's a down for you, Ken. 'Cos there's a lot to bein' in our clan.' Theo was standing still for once, staring into Kaninda's face, his attitude as if he'd got him by the collar. 'Belonging's good. There's strength, an' mates, an' people to take your side. Brothers an' sisters. Bein' in's a real good feeling; pos-it-ive! What you need in London, man.'

Kaninda put his hands in his pockets and walked away, told himself to stay calm so that he could fight the long battle, the wait. He had two objectives; kill N'gensi, and return to Lasai and kill all the other Yusulu he could. But to do these things he had to be in control of himself, had to fight the urge to shout at this Theo or run wild at N'gensi in the yard.

In the tutor group he dutifully returned what he had been given the day before – a permission slip signed by Mrs Captain Betty Rose allowing him to go outside the school that week for a lesson visit; the one the rude boy had been forbidden to make. Tate and Lyle: a factory: a refinery, for the purpose of studying production processes. Well, if that was what they did here he would have to do it, it was part of the war waiting. But it was something different he would be doing: dead Teacher Setzi would never sanction a visit, even to the lavatories. If it had to happen in lesson time, you came back to the room to have your bottom wiped by Big Master.

But as he had expected, there was more than the permission slip to talk about this morning – after the day before. He went to the desk with it and

Miss Mascall spoke to him privately while the rest of the class behaved like carnival.

'Now listen,' she said – 'And shut up Jon Bennett! – Kaninda, we've got Catholics here, and Jews, and Jehovah's Witnesses, and Salvation Army and God's Force. We've got Indians and Pakistanis and Sikhs; Hindus, Moslems, kids from this patch and that; we've got Somalis, Chinese, Vietnamese and some English, God help us. We've got gays, bi's and straights, and we've got Jon Bennett. And we don't bring any of that into school, except to celebrate our differences. In school we're here to learn, so if you want to stay and benefit you're going to make damned sure nothing like yesterday happens again. Right?'

Kaninda's face had gone rock hard, everything held inside, the features closed to the other's eye. *What did she know*?

'Do you understand?'

Still no crack, and the room had lost its noise.

'Kaninda, I know about Kibu and Yusulu. I see the news, read the papers. I understand. It's my *subject...*'

'It's my life!' Kaninda cracked where Sergeant Matu would never have cracked, not for such a dog whine of pity. He was straight away sorry that he'd opened his mouth to show such a soft inside.

'Well, I've warned you. You behave like the rest of us in school or you do the other thing.'

Kaninda didn't know what that other thing was; but he knew when a reprimand was over. He turned, drill style, and walked back to his seat.

'That's told 'im!' Jon Bennett called out. 'I make you right, Miss, 'cos we're all one big happy family, ain't we?' The class cheered.

To which Miss Mascall said, 'Bollocks!' and restored order; while Kaninda sat at his desk and stared at a reader without seeing the words.

It was an 'L' ambush; not in a straight line, not 'V' and not 'pinwheel', where you don't know which direction the enemy is coming from. It was at a bend in the road, with one of the assault platoons facing the Yusulu vehicles head-on and the other lying in wait at the side. When the convoy of trucks and carriers arrived in the killing zone the tug would be given and fire power poured on.

It was an up-country road, where the puddles and the potholes made steering columns the hardest working parts of the vehicles, where after such ambushes they said dead drivers could be picked out by the muscles in their arms. From a long way back the Yusulu ammunition convoy had revved and squeaked and kicked up red dust like a sunset – from his support position in a mound of wild cane Kaninda had seen it coming for half an hour.

And, like waiting for the worst always does, that half an hour seemed to take a day. Ants, flies, and aedes mosquitoes had him wriggling to shift his ground position without breaking cover or making any rustle that a Yusulu patrol might hear. His eyes down along the muzzle, Kaninda got high on the smell of lubricating oil and metal barrel hotting up in the sun.

Sergeant Matu wasn't far, but Kaninda didn't know where. Once he'd been put in his position before dawn, Kaninda could have been the only living thing in the African bush – apart from the insects – and now that living red dust of the convoy coming... It was lie still and chew spring bark – until the shooting had finished, when he'd have to be up and signing the way out for the assault platoons, along the underside of the ridge and down to the river where the boats were waiting. And, when Sergeant Matu gave the order, Kaninda's platoon would follow, turning and loosing off bursts in their strict arcs every twenty steps, in case any Yusulu had survived and come chasing. No chances! Sergeant Matu said.

Closer and closer came the sound of the vehicles in their kicked-up cloud, with the black exhaust of banged-out engines darkening the red dust. It was frightening, the relentless squeaking and revving of the approach, and Kaninda's heart was shaking his gun barrel, his throat drier than a mouthful of moth, the sweat of his face slipping his dark glasses down his nose.

Crunch, squeak, rev, backfire. Then, CRACK! And suddenly it started. Kaninda could hear it all happening, a hundred metres away: the detonations as Claymore mines sprayed steel balls into vehicles and men, the explosions as petrol tanks and ammunition went up in thick plumes, and loudest of all, the screams of dying Yusulu. And, fear being fear, when the first shots fired, they jumped Kaninda off the ground and he messed himself, crouching.

'Shit body! Shit Yusulu!' shouted inside his head. But it served a purpose. By cursing the Yusulu and his own running guts he was making himself angry as the smell of it outstank his fear. He jumped to his feet, ready to direct the assault platoons to the river.

'Stand! You got me? Stand!'

Now Kaninda knew where Sergeant Matu was, on the ridge above them, commanding his platoon to hold their positions, in place himself to shoot any man who didn't.

And as suddenly as it had begun, the shooting ended, unplugging the sounds of destruction, of death and of dying. But these were Yusulu sounds – and Kaninda's head jabbed in a fierce nod of pleasure that they were louder than even his mother's and father's and little Gifty's screams had been.

Till within seconds the assault platoons started running through with weapons slung. Forget the crap, Kaninda signalled them on, while over the ridge and below at the river the escape craft were starting up their outboards. But Kaninda's ears were still drawn to the screaming of the ambush zone, even after the last assault soldier had gone through. This was what he was here for.

Sergeant Matu blew his whistle. Kaninda and the back-up platoon could follow. Kaninda swung to go – just as he caught sight of another runner, coming shrieking – with wild eyes and burning hair, beating at himself, running at Kaninda.

Yusulu.

Kaninda knew what he had to do. Strangely calm and cold, the trained rebel fighter, he threw his M16 up to his shoulder and aimed – the head would be best but the belly was bigger. The burning

Yusulu saw what was happening and tried to weave, but Kaninda had his cheek welded to the stock and he shut his eyes and shot – not short and controlled but a spray of fire like a scribble across the man. Scribble, scribble, scribble him out. And before Kaninda knew what was happening, Sergeant Matu had scragged him from behind, clapped him on the back, and was pushing him along the ridge to slide him down to the river.

It wasn't until he was in a reed bed an hour later, washing out his trousers, that the shaking started.

He had killed a man. Whoever had started it, there was blood on his hands, too. The first of the blood.

CHAPTER NINE

Laura went back to the scene of the crime – because she desperately needed to know. Up to now her life had always been one great knowing – about God's power and the redeeming love of the Lord Jesus Christ, and about her place in Heaven at the end of things. Even her stupid rebellion had only been about testing these things she knew – and see where that had got her! Now she needed to know for certain what it was she had done; she had to measure the size of her sin. It was big, that was for sure. Already, some lowlife from Ropeyard Road had given little Jackson a kicking – but knowing the state of her victim was for Laura's peace right now.

What had happened had spun Laura's world out of control, although having Kaninda in the house did disguise it from the others. He had changed the atmosphere by taking her mother's know-all eyes off her daughter's distress – her not talking much, her never laughing these days, her forever tapping her knife at the table in a drummer's spasm. Laura knew what she was doing and just let it happen – because she could put everything down to suddenly having to cope with this boy in the house. Like her going out tonight – and besides, anyone would understand a girl of her age at this time of the month moodying off out of the house after she'd done her homework. So tonight was a good night for Laura to try to *know*.

In jeans and a dowdy top – so as not to draw attention – she walked to the near end of Ropeyard Road, walked fast as if she had a dog she was taking to the common, as if she were going somewhere. But her eyes loitered and her ears were bat sharp. In her wildest hope she wanted to pass a doorway and hear someone say, 'Good job that little girl's better – lucky it wasn't nothing serious...'

But she didn't. She hardly passed a soul to hear anything. Doors were shut, televisions flickered out blue – the place was all closed up for the evening; not even a cat on a wall to arch its back at this wicked witch. She walked one deserted street after another until she found herself at a couple of shops making a poor parade; a fish and chip shop and a late store where stock was spaced out to make the shelves look full.

A kid walked into the fish and chip shop, started losing money loudly in the arcade machine; otherwise there was no life here, either. Laura pretended to read the menu prices on the window while she went over everything again.

What did they know about the accident, she and Theo? They knew the car had hit the little girl – but Laura had no 'feel' for a steering wheel so she didn't know how hard it had hit; then the next had been the police going looking round the estates for a car without plates. That was all she knew. She didn't know the state of the kid they'd hit – an ear to the ground at school had only come up with dirt – and Theo didn't seem to care. So was the girl alive or dead, would she be back at school by the end of the week or was a funeral planned? Laura shivered at the thought; but she did need to know. How could she pray to God for forgiveness until she knew what she had to be forgiven for?

Which was when Laura saw the newspaper rack on the late shop door. One faded *Daltons' Weekly* and today's local newspaper, the *Thames Reach Trader*: when she saw what she needed to know printed in heavy black. Banner headline. And Laura's renewed faith in the Lord suddenly had to face up to its first big test – because that headline was telling her that He wasn't going to be kind to this sinner.

*

No one much was ever kind to Sharon Slater so she had secrets the way other people have friends, or pets, or hobbies. Secrets were what she was all about, because that was how she got by with her father and Auntie Dove, her new mother: a secret life to make up for the real one. And sharing a room called for the best-kept secrets of all – but Sharon was up to it. She made her own bed each morning, not to be helpful but to cover any accident in the night. Her secret. That way she suffered only one smack in seven, on a Sunday when the sheets were changed.

But her most dangerous secret would have got her more than a slap on the leg – the hidden photograph of herself and her real mother, taken one happy seaside day, the two of them squeezed heads together, in a photo booth – which she kept in a variety of places where Auntie Dove's girl Michelle wouldn't find it; right now in a box of tissues. And she'd hidden the number plate the kids hadn't thrown into the river along the top shelf of her side of the cupboard, under the newspaper lining; stolen and kept because the letters of her mother's name shone off it – G34 MLS – Marlene Leigh Slater; a secret that seemed to burn in there when the letterbox clattered and Sharon read the headline of the *Thames Reach Trader* pushed through.

HIT AND RUN. EVIL OF THE CAR WITH NO PLATES. No plates?! Mouth open, she started reading the report on the front page.

> *Little Dorothy Hedges was running an everyday errand for her mother when she was brutally hit by a car in Ropeyard Road, Thames Reach. Now she's in hospital fighting for her life. The suspect car was red and carried no licence plates – though from the one word the child has said in her coma the driver was white.*

Sharon stopped; a tight frown on her face.

> *Dorothy's mother Mrs Rene Hedges said, 'I'm well annoyed. I want this villain caught. I can't rest till I face out the brute who's done this to my Dolly.'*

'You reading again?' Auntie Dove coming out of nowhere snatched the paper from Sharon, took it into the kitchen and threw it on the draining board. 'The time for reading's when the work's done!' And she tossed a dishcloth at her. 'Dream machine, you c'n look a bit useful, miss!'

But it's hard for someone to look useful when their brain's battling with the unbelievable, when they're onto a secret that blows the mind. Sharon did her best, but she still ended up with a clout.

*

For Laura it was the stomach drop, the ice cold skin, the asthmatic panic of there being no air to breath on. The little girl now had a name, a name she would never forget, and in the way most names do, it straight off brought an image with it. *Dolly Hedges. Dolly* – small, raggish, floppy little arms and legs; *Hedges* – bedraggled, dusty, the sort of thing you come through backwards. Standing there dry mouthed, Laura could see quite clearly this scruffy little scrap with her untidy fair hair, grey-blue eyes – and lying limp in the gutter. The child who had caught enough of a glimpse of her to give a description...

Standing there in the street, she tried to hold the paper as if all she'd bought it for was the local lottery result, but as her eyes stared till they made a dizzy nonsense of the words on the page, her Christian heart knew that this news called for only one thing now – a full confession, a completely clean breast made of it. She took a step, sat on a wall. Except – she wasn't in this on her own, was she? Her confession would have to take into account the fact of who'd driven the car off in the first place, who'd told her she could have a go at the wheel of his brother's car.

So she didn't go home. After sitting there till

the stonework chilled up into her, she went from Ropeyard Road direct to the Barrier – where Mal was fitting new wiper blades to his car. To *that car*. That devil's car. Laura had seen it so many times in her head, in those never-ending thoughts about what had happened, now she saw again for real the interior, the seat where she'd sat and its pattern, the steering wheel she hadn't twisted fast enough, the gearstick which had started things off. And because she was drawn to it like someone hypnotised, she saw clearest of all the front near-side, the headlight, the part of the bodywork that had hit little Dolly Hedges: where there was no mark, no scratch, no dent to show what had happened. And all in the space of five seconds her eyes went to the bumper and its number plate.

'How many number plates does cars have?'

'Eh?'

It was Sharon Slater asking the question, come from nowhere, but not asking Mal, asking her.

''Lo Sharon? Read your prize gospel yet?'

'"Saint John"? Bit *good*, i'n he? Been reading, though...'

'Yeah?'

'The *Trader*. I like the news about round here, it's more...like, real.'

Laura nodded, a weak movement on a frail neck.

'So, how many?' Sharon persisted.

'Is this a car quiz? We could run a quiz one night at God's Force if you like...'

'I'll tell you, they got two. One plate on the front an' one on the back.'

'That's the law, isn't it?'

'Because this car's got three. It had four, there was one left behind, on that wall. An' there's these two on it now...' She pointed to one of them, the plate at the front.

Mal looked up, but he didn't seem to have caught much of this. He looked interested, though, so Laura drew Sharon away.

'What *are* you on about, Sha?'

'Tell you what, I'll look this way. I'll look out across the river at Tates's.' She turned herself to face towards the ship across the Thames and the refinery quay where it was unloading. 'An' I'll tell you the number of that red car there...'

'Is this a trick, or something...?' But Laura knew what it was, she had too good an idea of what was coming.

'The number of that car is G34 MLS.'

'Clever. So?'

'My mum's letters of her name. Her birthday when she went off, and her name.'

'Ah. What a coincidence.' Laura had never been the fainting sort, but right now she had to lean casually on the riverside rail in case she went down.

'I know that number 'cos I've got that plate at home. I nicked it, off that wall when they went in for their dinner. Left the other one, but I nicked one, so I know it ain't on that car. Those on it have got to be new.'

'Well, they'd have to be, if you nicked one of their others.' A try, but Sharon knew, Sharon knew...

'Yeah, you're right.' With which Sharon went; left matters there, and went.

Laura opened her mouth to suck in the cold air off the river. She was hot, in a sweat, and as weak as if she hadn't eaten for a month; and her inside pained her with more than with her period.

'Is Theo in?' she found herself asking Mal.

Mal gave her a look and a bit of a smile; he pulled a mobile out of his shirt pocket and tapped in a number. 'Theo? Get down 'ere, man, you got a call-out.'

Laura could hear Theo's voice from there, river breeze or no; but not the words. Mal was looking at her, clearly lost for how to describe her to Theo while she was listening.

'Tell him it's Laura, and she's not going away.'

'It's Laura, an' she 'ain't budgin' till you're on the spot.' Mal snapped the phone shut, nodded at her, got on with the fiddle of the wiper blade.

Within minutes Theo was walking across the paving with a mile-high bounce in his step, way above, whipping his fingers and acting so cool it was a miracle the Thames didn't freeze over. Real *sool*.

'Lau-ra! Pos-it-ive! What you doin' down here? I'm up to there wi' Technology homework...' Without stopping he grabbed her arm and bounced her away from Mal and along to where the Thames Barrier children's playground stood deserted. He sat on a swing. 'What's givin', girl?'

'You seen the paper?'

'Charlton Afletic's goin' down?'

'The *Trader*, the front page, about the accident, the little girl.'

'I did see somethink.'

'*Something*? Did you see that she's in a coma?'

'Is that the word? Thought it was comma, like, halfway to a full-stop...'

'Yeah, and I think she might be, as it happens. More than halfway.'

'Saw it.' Theo started to swing, but straight away scraped his trainers to stop. 'Lor, what's to say we done it, man?'

Laura grabbed the chains of his swing, held him there. 'There's *everything* to say we done it. Red car, no plates – which it didn't have, and certain people *know* it didn't have – and did you read the only word Dolly Hedges said?'

'Gi's a clue.'

'She said, "white".' Laura took off a hand to thump her own chest. 'That means me. She was describing the driver.'

'Nah. "White"? Rules you out; you *an'* me. I'm black as Jamaican pride, an' you're sort of—'

'Could be white to someone in a rush.'

Theo looked at her in the hazy red of a setting sun, up river over London.

'I'm light, aren't I?'

'Bein' black don' pay off much round here, so be light, girl, be white as you can.'

Laura let go his swing, sat on another and started a small rocking motion without her feet leaving the ground.

'In Seychelles Creole there's no word for "racism", you know that? When you're born they're interested in your colour only like they're interested in whether you're a girl or a boy – they reckon it's just as nice either way, or in-between. But round here it's the first thing that goes on a police description' She turned round to face him. 'They'll get us, Theo – so what are you going to do about it?'

'*Us*?'

Laura swung round to hit him, on a forward rock. 'Don't come that! You were in that car! You drove it off. I know, and I know someone else who knows.'

'Who?'

'Some kid.'

Theo thought about it. 'We'd go down,' he said. 'They put you away for that sort of thing. Def-in-ite.'

'But what if we went in and confessed, didn't wait for them to find us, said we were sorry as soon as we found out what happened...'

Theo pondered on. 'Sort o' thing might help a bit with the ol' judge...' He stood up, threw the swing back in an angry twist. 'It's what the Federation's gonna do you got to worry about! Told you before. There's gonna be a war, an' you'll be first target, an' me next.'

Laura stopped his swing from hitting her, faced the Thames. 'Right now I'd just as soon jump in that river. I'm ready for that, Theo.'

'Neg-a-tive, you're not! Not when we got plans...'

'What plans?'

Theo was back to looking cocky. 'I ain't just been listenin' to you, swinging here. I been thinking.' He used his fingers, one, two. 'We beat the Federation – we get your Ken an' his tricks an' all of us, and we *do* them, Baz Rosso's working on it. An' when they're out the picture, sorted – *then* we go an' see Old Bill...'

Laura frowned. 'You'll go – with me?'

Theo showed her his palms. 'Is my name Theo Julien?'

'It's what you told me.'

'Be pos-it-ive, girl! You gotta have trust.' Theo jumped onto the seat of his swing and started working up high. 'You get Ken down here tomorrow night to see Baz, an' we'll go from there.'

Laura's eyes swung with him. 'Is that a promise, then, a deal? I get you Kaninda, and when you've had your war we go to the police? Both of us?'

Theo whooped at her. 'Less I c'n think of a better way.'

'Shake on it?'

'Kiss on it.'

'I'm not into that any more.'

'All right, shake on it. When I come down.'

So when he came down they shook on it, with Theo suddenly tight in the face again as if his stomach had really turned over tonight, and not on account of the swinging.

CHAPTER TEN

Two school buses dropped them off at Tate and Lyle's; Kaninda's class with Miss Mascall and another class with the big teacher who had stopped Kaninda strangling Faustin N'gensi. He was keeping as fierce an eye on Kaninda as Teacher Setzi during an examination, never blinking. With reason. Every minute, every moment, every breath he took, Kaninda's mind was obsessed with this enemy. In his sleep he strangled him, butchered him, riddled him with bullets. In the day he watched him, always knowing where the Yusulu was, what track he'd taken – which classroom, what lesson. N'gensi was not going to be transferred quietly to some other school without Kaninda knowing because he was the target, he was the walking dead. And that morning the whereabouts of Kaninda seemed to have Faustin's whole time attention too, going by his eyes and the twisting of his neck. But not for long, because the two groups split for their tours of the factory – of the refinery – one group going to the company museum first while Kaninda's began the tour.

'We're here to see an industrial process,' Miss Mascall told them. 'In at one end – off the ship – out at the other, onto the backs of lorries, all in fifteen hours.'

'I'm goin' bowling tonight!' one of the girls complained.

'The *process* takes fifteen hours, not our visit! Who'd want to spend the night with you?'

'Me, Miss – I'll spend the night with her!'

'You'd be lucky, Thacker!'

And so on, from their first arrival into the reception area where they were taken over by Mr McNab of the Tate and Lyle staff – and expertly shut up by him with a surprise command.

'Anyone wearing a watch, take it off and put it in your pocket. Anyone wearing a ring, likewise. Put on those white coats hanging by there – and also the wee hairnet you'll find in the pocket...'

'Do what?'

'*Hairnet*? He think I'm a nance?'

'Haste along, then, we don't have all day.' The man himself led the way to a white coat and a hairnet, slipping his watch in his pocket as he went. Kaninda went with the rest, but wore no ring and had never had a watch. His father's had been smashed by bullets, and he hadn't had the courage to claim the wedding ring off the mash of his fingers.

'No one wants your dandruff or your Rolex in their packet of sugar...'

Kaninda was slipping into a white coat. *Sugar*? The word stopped him, one arm in, one arm out. *Sugar*? There'd been no thought in his head except Yusulu, he was walking through this visit like a Bantu ghost – but this was sugar? Jostled, he found his hairnet in a plastic bag in the pocket – and heard none of the commotion as the others had hysterics at the sight of one another putting them on. *Sugar*? He knew about sugar. He'd hidden with Sergeant Matu and the platoon in the giant grass which was sugar cane, and at the Mozambique border he'd seen it up close till he was weary with seeing the stems running with big ants, felt the sharp prick of the leaf ends when he moved carelessly. He'd seen loving in sugar, killing in sugar: sugar was sweet to most; to him it was rancid in the mouth.

But they were moving on, the man talking fast so the front few could hear, Miss Mascall repeating what she heard for the rest. Kaninda followed, his mind starting to yield to some other thought now than killing N'gensi. He stood with the rest as they marvelled at the mountain of raw brown sugar in its huge shed, were bored by the machines which spun out the impurities in water vapour centrifuges, and lined up to wash their hands before going in to where the automatic system weighed bright white sugar and discharged it into the packets they saw being folded and formed in front of their eyes; coming off the conveyor belt in big, plastic-wrapped consignments, printed up in Arabic, Swahili and English.

In *Swahili*? His mouth had suddenly gone so dry he found it hard to ask the question.

'Not for England, just?'

Mr McNab was pleased to get it. 'Oh, no, sonny. This little lot's going back where it came from. Refined, for the cities...'

'Cities?'

'Beira, Maputo...In Mozambique.'

Kaninda made a note on his clipboard, to keep his head down and his face hidden.

'So now you've seen the whole process,' Miss Mascall told the class. 'As I said, fifteen hours from unloading to despatch.'

'Although it takes a full week to unload a big ship,' Mr McNab was going on. 'Which leads us outside...' His schools' tour of the Tate and Lyle refinery ended with the beginning of the process, going out to see the huge ship at the quay, having the raw sugar sucked from its holds. All of which was being noted by Kaninda, not on paper but the way he took instructions from Sergeant Matu – in his soldier's brain. '*You got me*?' Kaninda wanted to raise his fist in salute.

Outside on the quay the other teacher's class had been waiting. With N'gensi. Kaninda ducked as his party threaded their way along water-greened walkways, climbed runged stairs. Emerging onto the same quayside, they saw a long sunken rail which ran like a tramway about a metre from the edge. It made a good off-limits line for safety. Faustin N'gensi's class was ranged along it looking at the sugar ship; and, like most off-limits lines, it was being tested with feet stepping over it.

'I told you, no nearer!' the teacher shouted.

But the Yusulu was standing close enough to touch the ship's side – or to fall between the quay and the ship into the sucking water.

Kaninda estimated it was ten metres to his target – as a girl pulled N'gensi back from the edge.

'He can't swim, sir.'

'So, what do you want, a George Medal?' the deputy head asked.

'The holds are all but empty,' Mr McNab told Kaninda's class – as the other group headed in to see the processing. 'Then she'll make her return trip...'

Which shot Kaninda's mind off N'gensi. 'To Maputo, going?' he asked.

'Aye, to Maputo. On the Saturday night tide. You remembered. You've got a bright lad here, Miss Mascall.'

'Oh, yes,' she said, smiling.

And Kaninda was smiling, too. Not on his face, to show, but inside. This ship was going back to Mozambique. Soon...

Laura wasn't sure how to go about it. She knew how she could get Theo to follow her like some hungry dog; she could always make his eyes sparkle big if she looked at him straight and showed him the quick tip of her tongue; she'd see him swallow, working up for the kiss he was being promised. But a boy like Kaninda – there couldn't be any of that with him. All the same, she had to deliver him to Theo that evening or there was no chance the slippery eel would ever keep his part of the bargain.

So, how? What got Kaninda going? He never said much at home, just followed along where it suited him – like mending the chairs at God's Force or walking with her to school; sat quiet in an armchair and stared at the TV like someone in a mental ward; or he lay on his bed in his room. Sometimes he'd shout in his sleep, but his face when he was awake never showed any emotion. There was a word for it – traumatised; making slits of his eyes and staring at you, not moving any other muscle.

Pathetic, sad Kaninda. It didn't take much knowing why. He'd seen his mother and his father and his little sister massacred and been lucky to be left for dead himself – so was it any wonder the boy couldn't get excited about anything here in England?

Or was that true? He had got excited over one thing, hadn't he – that other new African boy in the school. He'd gone for him crazy in the school corridor, had to be pulled off by the teachers, got excited enough about someone from the enemy side in his civil war. No big surprise – that had to be where his mind was fixed.

No, no big surprise – and she'd got it! Without messing, Laura was tapping on Kaninda's bedroom door within seconds, a secret sort of tap, not the bang and blow-on-in of her mother. There was no 'Come in' or anything of that; but after a wait there was a cautious opening of the door and Kaninda's head – well, more like one eye – came round it.

'Kaninda—' Laura kept her voice on the level of conspiracy – 'that African kid at school...'

The widened eye invited more.

'That other refugee from Lasai...' The door opened a fraction wider; now there was the other eye.

But Laura stopped. What was she doing? She turned her head away. She was only about to lie to Kaninda about the other kid being down at the Barrier right now with Theo! *To lie*. Not only that, but lie because she knew Kaninda had a grudge and wanted to hurt him, badly. So was Laura Rose down to dealing in hate, when she had no part in their war, took no side? How low had she sunk?

'What?'

'Oh, nothing.'

Kaninda frowned at her, the door went back to one eye's width. She'd lost him, but she had to have him – some other way.

'Want to come out tonight? You and me, just for a walk?' Suddenly she was vamping now. 'Only, I don't know you, you don't know me. Just an hour, down by the river, where you like to be? Get to know each other...'

Kaninda angled his head; and in spite of herself, Laura didn't know why, she flashed him the tip of her tongue, the quickest flick, it could have been nerves.

And the door opened, Kaninda came quietly out.

'Like, you and me, sort of, family,' Laura corrected.

And Kaninda still followed.

It was the river that had been in Kaninda's head when the tap came on the door; the river, with the ship from Mozambique tied up at the sugar quay. N'gensi, short plan. Ship, long plan. He had been lying there seeing the waterline running wet along her hull, picturing the froth of her prow cutting white through the ocean; right then thinking that he wanted to see this ship again, to sort some things in his mind – when, like a partisan coming out of the bush, this Laura was at his door talking about going where he wanted, and saving him from creeping out of the house like a soldier going to the village for a girl. And in her talk had been something of the Yusulu N'gensi; she had started and stopped about him.

So, was the target going to be there, too?

But what was that she'd done quickly with her tongue, like the convent girls did when the nuns weren't looking, looking like she was *enticing*? He did what boys did, but he didn't want girl business; all that dandling did was weaken soldiers, took them off their edge; and he needed to be steely and sharp until the war was won.

But he did want another look at that ship; and if N'gensi *might* be at the river...

'This is Baz Rosso.'

But the Yusulu wasn't. There was Theo and a bigger white boy, more of a man, but no N'gensi. The two were sitting high on the back of a wooden seat near the children's playground where Theo had said the Crew test was run.

The man flicked a cigarette butt across the pathway and over into the water. Kaninda walked on past the two of them to the river rail and leant on the smooth wooden top. He didn't know for sure what he'd come for, but he had not come for this.

'It's good stuff I'm hearing about you, Ken.'

Give no answer. Kaninda went on looking across and down river at where the sugar was being sucked out of the long ship.

'Theo tells, like, you're some mondo fighter.'

So was it going back to that? Theo and his Crew tribe, his war? He had given his answer to Theo, and it would do for this man, too – which was negative, best told by saying nothing.

'You got a tongue, have you?'

Kaninda turned slowly to face the man and

showed it to him. He showed it to Laura, too, in no way like she'd shown hers to him. There were going to be no mistakes.

'Same colour as mine.' But Baz Rosso's eyes seemed to be weighing up the worth of going on wasting time talking to this kid.

'Ken, this guy can help you.' Theo was quickly over to Kaninda. 'What you want? Puff, skunk, super skunk, any of that tripping stuff – you had that over Africa – he can get all that, can't you, Baz?' Theo was acting like someone who'd delivered an ox but it wouldn't pull, so he was trying a tickle first. He dropped his voice from Laura. 'Or Jane? Baz can fix you up with a girl, any colour, any time.'

'Or N'gensi, can you get me?' Kaninda had spoken.

'N'gensi?'

'*You* get me?' It was Theo Kaninda was speaking to.

'Pos-it-ive. You jus' got to do the run, it's the rules, an' then Crew brothers help Crew brothers. Anythink they want...'

Kaninda ran his hand along the wooden rail top, because he had seen where the tide level was at this time in the evening – it was low, and the rocks and stones were showing wicked beneath. But with low or high tide, it made no difference if Faustin

N'gensi could not swim: and him dying in an initiation rite would bring no police hands on Kaninda's shoulder – that would be accident, like a bad soldier shot while the corporal was cleaning his gun.

Kaninda turned back to Theo, still ignored this Baz. 'So you get Lasai boy? See if he does this.'

'Yeah, I can do anythink, Ken. Whenever. The more the better. This time tomorrow?'

Kaninda nodded sharp.

'But only when *you're* in the Crew, man.'

Kaninda looked out at the river again, then cast his eye along the line of the wooden rail top. 'I do this,' he suddenly said.

'Top dog!'

'What? I didn't know... I wouldn't have...' Laura put her hand to her mouth, and closed her eyes.

Theo took Kaninda back along the walkway to its beginning, where it met the Thames Barrier wall. As they strode out the metres Kaninda saw the tall buildings of the city up river, heard a small jet making a roar of a landing somewhere over on his right; looked up at the red lights on the nearest Barrier pier.

'Got your apple, Ken?'

Kaninda turned the slits of his eyes onto Theo. He *had* boasted about the short time he would take to run this rail, with time to eat an apple. Now he looked back along the hundred metres of narrow wooden top and all those round bosses like cow dung that had to be got over between the sections of railing. It was a long run back to the play zone where the girl Laura and the man Baz were standing.

'I'll run with you, man, down here on the path.'

Kaninda said nothing. He took off the black school shoes Mrs Captain Betty Rose had bought him – he still wore no socks – and pulled himself up onto the smooth rail top to face the run. For a few moments he balanced and calmed himself, thought of Sergeant Matu shouting at the men to breath deep before running in a fast attack. '*Pump up! Pump up! You got me?*' So Kaninda pumped up. He had run over rope bridges across ravines and dead trees across water; such running took breath for the speed and stamina, and no fuzziness in the head for not losing the footing. Oxygen, it took. Now this hard, straight run on smooth wood was not so difficult; but there were the round bosses sticking up; and a stepping out along the first section showed it to be too short for three strides, too long for two. So, pump up! pump up! for speed and for fast blood to give clear eyes. The stones and rocks so far below would not leave much of anyone alive.

But he would look along, not down. Even from here he could see the man Baz checking his watch as he held his other arm high for the signal, with Laura standing beside him at the rail.

'You reckon N'gensi could do this an' all?' Theo asked.

Kaninda ignored him. He did *not* think so: he would drown, or be killed on the stones, which was the only reason Kaninda Bulumba was doing it; having the Yusulu here tomorrow to fail and fall.

'Be hot, Ken! Thirty seconds, man.'

And now nothing else was in Kaninda's mind than that arm the man had raised along there. Pant the breath now, and no blinks.

So, go! The arm swept down and Kaninda pushed off, eyes on the feet, on the length, up and down – feet, length – as he found the paces, straight and fast, angling his body to the land side, arms out for balance. Two strides, a half stride, step the boss; two strides, a half stride, step the boss; two and a half, step; two and a half, step – then eyes ahead on the target finish as he hit a fast rhythm with balance, balance, balance like a commando on a wall. There was a breeze trying to blow him off but he could put on pace for that, and the acceleration gave him a longer stride so that ten bosses along he was two-ing, two-ing, two-ing. Thirty seconds would be easy – he could have brought the apple – like running the chase when the Yusulu patrol caught them at the mission eating fruit, when he'd had to get away with the panic of a bullet coming in his back, his heart and lungs never working so hard, his feet and eyes never so fiercely concentrated on the stepping; foot here, foot there, over stumps, through gaps, pounding the red earth and running, running, running; till the Yusulu had lowered their rifles, clattered to a stop, and he had found his half-eaten apple squashed to pip and pulp in his hand. Now it was the same but easier; the drop was always below but there was no bullet at his back.

Ten bosses to go, nine bosses; two and step, two and step; seven bosses, six, five, four, three, two – and Theo shouting at him, Laura staring.

'Great, Ken! You're sool, you!'

One boss—

Yusulu? What was that Theo shouted? N'gensi was here?

The last boss, but a flash of lost eye and a toe too low – and in his confusion Kaninda tripped, staggered, tried to regain his balance but went crashing along the rail top, his body on the river side and his hands flailing for a grip but getting none, the smooth wood denying him.

Over! Going down to the rocks! No saving him – except for two hands suddenly grabbing, gripping with a tight hurt but holding him, just – till other hands came and checked him, dangling, to hard haul him back over the rail top and onto the pathway like a landed croc.

'Pos-it-ive, Laura, you was quick!'

Theo and the man Baz had pulled him over and safe; but the first there, the saving hands, had been Laura's.

Kaninda looked up at her. He said nothing; nodded; nodded his acknowledgement as comrades do: *I owe you my life! I owe you!*

They brushed him down, hard.

'Vincitore! You made it –' the man Baz told him, '– the feet was into the final section inside the due time.'

Theo whooped. 'You're in, Ken, you're in the Crew! See?'

Baz Rosso walked away, as if generals didn't wait listening to foot soldiers' talk; but, over his shoulder: 'Tomorrow, when I find out more what I need to know, we talk tactics and strategy.'

'N'gensi,' was all Kaninda could say – to Theo. 'Yusulu.'

'Sure, Ken, pos-it-ive!'

'Here. You get him.'

Theo frowned. 'What for? For Crew?'

'Me and that boy, just.'

'Any way you want, Ken 'cos you're in!' Theo made no sudden move – no one made a sudden move at Kaninda – but he leant forward and put his hands to Kaninda's trouser belt. 'Your belt, man...'

'So?'

He gave it a sideways pull, set the buckle off-centre, to the right. 'Now you're Crew.'

'How?'

'Crew display. Seen Baz's belt – and mine?'

Kaninda looked. Theo's belt buckle was off-centre, to the right. 'Crew c'n tell Crew, but not no one else...'

Kaninda pulled the buckle back dead centre. '*I* know. Enough.'

And Theo was taken away by Laura, him looking like wanting to put an arm round her and her holding him off.

Which left Kaninda staring down at the drop he'd missed only by the speed and strength of that girl. He had been spared, he had not joined his ghost with his mother's and his father's and little Gifty's; not yet. He had been spared because still he had things to do, still there was a war to fight.

Which led his eye up from the foreshore and across river to the ship again. The sugar ship to Mozambique. The ship which the man had said sailed on the Saturday night tide.

CHAPTER ELEVEN

Prowling the Millennium Mall was warmer than standing in the river breeze which blew along the Thames Reach streets. Like the river, the shopping mall was at the northern end of the town centre that separated the Barrier Estate from the Ropeyard streets. But it wasn't the nip that took Snuff Bowditch in there, it was the nick. Easy game! There were two floors of Oxford Street stores for Security to patrol, and he'd had Security's movements timed since he could tie his own shoes. There was always a seven minute period when both sets of security men were on the same floor, and getting up or down on the escalator was slow work with all the moron shoppers. Each big store had its own people and its cameras, but they were window dressing to someone like Snuff. What he did was, he wore what everyone wore – jeans, dirty trainers, dingy top with a bit of length – no roses in his buttonhole or purple shirts to stand him out – and he moved fast and he kept his head down. It was how Snuff funded his habits so this was work to him, a pro job. He didn't cruise around sussing this and that, then do the nick. He did his choosing a day or so before, when he could be wearing a ballerina's skirt and no knickers – let 'em look, he wasn't doing anything wrong. Then he came back later for what he wanted; shirts, jumpers, reefers, coats, kiddies' clothes, the stuff people needed. Forget electricals, clothes was best, nothing to go wrong – it fits 'em or it don't. Ready money, in his hand.

Tonight was one of those look-see nights, seeing if Marks' still had car coats – for a bloke who'd left his other one in the pictures and daren't go back for it. If they had, Snuff would come back and do the business another day, choose one of the shifts when the spotty security was on who liked chatting up the cash-out girls. The coat went into a Marks' bag from Snuff's pocket, and he was out of the back door like diarrhoea.

But who did he see round the chocolate and sweets feeding *her* habit? Queen Max.

'Snuff!'

'Wotcha.'

'What you doin'?'

''Avin' a look. For Saturday.'

A Mountain Fudge went down Queen Max's top like Madam Miracle's magic show. 'Leave Saturday.'

'Yeah?'

'Word's out. Kicking-in that black kid. Baz Rosso wants a war – an' he goes snooker Saturdays, *an'* Charlton's at home, when Old Bill's gonna be well tucked up. So we'll hit 'em then.'

'Nice one.'

'I got brains.'

'No, nice fudge, my favourite. You wanna get it out quick, though, 'fore it melts.'

She eyed him. 'No problem. It's cold as ice, down there.'

'Yeah. I probly believe you...' And Snuff took a fudge, too, just to keep his hand in.

'Sweet Jesus, Lord, what next?'

Laura could be off her food but she still had to help get the supper. Tonight it was savoury tuna balls and mash. She was on the mash, peeling potatoes, while her mother was flaking tuna into a bowl of breadcrumbs and moulding it nimbly as if it were an old craft. By feel – her eye was on the local news coming out of the kitchen television.

'The trash who'd do such a devil thing!'

Laura had already just missed cutting a finger off. Now she put down the knife, for steadying herself.

'Joy-ridin' and knocking down a kid, an' all. Round here. An' driving off! What next, Lord, what next?'

Laura thought she might be sick, all over the supper. It was getting bigger all the time, the sin she'd committed. It was on television in everyone's kitchen now.

'Perhaps they didn't know what they did...'

Another tuna ball was thrown into the bowl, breaking with the force of it like a tuna grenade. '*Didn't know*? How could you didn't know you'd done such a thing like that? An' what was they doin' in the car in the first place? Racing round the streets with no identification marks! That car's not legal from the start...' She remade the tuna ball, then held the handle of the potato knife at Laura, with a look to say *get on*! '"Didn't know what they was doin'"! Lord have mercy! They knew, an' they deserve God's punishment, don't care who they are, I don' want them goin' up to my heaven, I tell you.' She looked to the ceiling, as if it were there. 'Anyhow, what's this "they"? I didn't hear no "they" about it...'

Now the potato knife clattered to the floor, and Laura bent to pick it up, thinking she could never come up again. Except, her mother had said it with a light touch, and now she was going on at the weather woman.

'Look at that make-up on her! And that blouse. Ain't she got no shame, paradin' herself like that in front of the nation?'

Somehow Laura finished the potatoes and made a homework excuse: but the way she felt she'd as soon have done what she'd told Theo, walked out of the front door, down to the river, and thrown herself over where Kaninda had nearly gone. Finish. Goodbye. Because, never mind the Ropeyard Federation, never mind the law – God and her own mother would wreak the greatest punishment on this wicked sinner. The Pope could excommunicate, and so could Captain Betty Rose: being a daughter wouldn't come into it up against being a sinner. There was no way Laura could turn, nowhere to go. Sharon Slater knew about it, probably Theo's Mal and Lydia as well, and now she'd nearly given herself away in classic criminal style. It was only a matter of time. What she desperately needed was to find a phone and talk to Childline or the Samaritans – or just have someone more responsible than Theo to be in it with.

She stood in her bedroom and stared into the mirror. She could easily look eighteen – and girls ran away to London, didn't they? What was Manchester like, or Glasgow? Couldn't she do it the other way round – run *from* London, and start a new life on the streets somewhere? Others did it, and she could look after herself.

And she'd have to – because where was God? She wanted to cry with the injustice of it. Tonight she'd stopped Kaninda falling to his death, she'd saved a life; tonight there was one more soul still alive because of her. But did that count? Did that go into God's scale pan? She twisted her face up at her bedroom ceiling, in the direction her mother reckoned Heaven was. If she could have spat as far as the gospel lampshade she'd have done it. She'd given God a second chance, she'd changed back from being a rebel and this was how He said thank-you. She'd prayed till her eyes ached with staying shut, she hadn't been able to find enough grovelling words to say how sorry she was, asking for a bit of compassion, a bit of hope – which was supposed to be His line, wasn't it? And, what? He knew she was going to do the right thing, He saw everything, He knew she'd done a deal with Theo to get all the right stuff done, by the law, by her everlasting soul. But what does He do? For a thank-you He gets on to South East Today!

She *was* crying now; on her bed, face down, smelling the Comfort in the duvet that was all the comfort she was going to find. Well, she'd been right to kick against God's Force: what she wore in secret, the kisses she gave Theo, any of the stuff that would have made her mum jump up and down shouting 'Jezebel!' – she'd been dead right, because there wasn't any God's justice the other way.

She got up from the bed – and straight off froze at a creak by her door. There was someone out there, going past, or coming bursting in! She held her breath as best she could in the sobbing, tried to put a look on her face someone else could see, made no sound, listened. But he'd gone on past. It must have been Kaninda, going downstairs.

And then she saw it: the bookshelf which ran along the top of the old fireplace, just to the left of the wardrobe. Her books were all out of order; her black writers weren't together – and she'd know because she'd put them there. And they were sloping over, loose not tight, as if some had been taken out. So what was missing? She tried to check, but she was in too much of a state to know what should have been there and what wasn't. Her diary? She kept a slim little diary among those books where her mother wouldn't find it – poems, silly confessions, words of favourite songs – he hadn't been at that, had he? Because she knew who'd been in her room. Kaninda. Her mother left her mark, by mouth – no way would she have been in this room and not had a go just now about her school uniform tossed in the corner on the floor. Her father wouldn't dare; he hardly dared go in his own bedroom. No, it had to be Kaninda who'd been on the snoop.

And he'd just gone downstairs. So, what was it he'd had? Well, there was a quick way of finding out.

Kaninda wasn't downstairs. Like Snuff Bowditch he was on the prowl – but not in Millennium Mall; he was up river beyond the Thames Barrier.

Close and distant, near and far – although not so distant, not so far now, he thought. Tomorrow he was going to take a revenge on Faustin N'gensi that was still making his mouth wet with wanting, throbbing his temples with action blood – but after that the getting back to the war would also be soon; or the starting of getting back, just, the hiding on the sugar ship going to Mozambique.

The atlas in the girl's room had shown him. The ship would go into the port of Maputo, or Beira; better if it was going on, then he would trek up country north across the border into Zimbabwe and through to Lasai. It would be a long trek but he might get lifts on roads and tracks, or even up the Limpopo River on a craft – and for not being captured he was trained to be as invisible as a spirit ghost.

These things were going well – but there was still a creasing in his stomach from before. He had been in big danger in the rebel army: he had only just escaped with his life when Sergeant Matu and the platoon had been killed; many times he had run from bullets and hidden where wild animals stalked – and on that terrible night at the start he had been left for dead in his own home, waiting for the bullets to kick into him, too. But tonight had been another time of strong danger – nearly killed, when only the hands of the girl had saved him from smashing down onto the rocks. And now he had a plan he wanted to live. He would salute her at some time before he went.

It was finding how he would cross the river to the ship. There was no way past the security on the land side, but across the river would take him direct to the walkways and steps of the refinery quayside, and there were no rat guards on the mooring lines, he'd seen. But he had also seen the current, he'd watched floating timber being carried up river faster than a man can walk. He couldn't swim it; but along a riverside weren't there always small boats? This was why he was here.

The river path took him to where factories stood on one side and the river the other. There were old jetties, rail lines going nowhere, conveyor belts running overhead where sand was carried off ships on to huge mounds, higher even than the raw sugar had been in the refinery. Below him the mud sucked and the rubbish of the world seemed trapped in little creeks and under wooden pilings. A dead cat lay where it had been left high by the tide, its fur partly gone, its tail as bald as a rat's.

He came round another bend where a line of houses stood facing the river, and alongside them was what he was looking for! A small boat, roped to the stern of something bigger with a cabin, the *'Argy Bargy'*, floating like a villager's boat on a tributary, the sort his Katonga friends would stand in and pole through the shallows looking for the eggs of river birds. There was no pole here – and a pole would be no good in this deep river – but among all the floating debris there would be wood for rough oars, plenty.

He looked beyond the *'Argy Bargy'* and saw more cabin boats tied to buoys not far out; some of them with dinghies at their sterns. Again, plenty. He looked down river through the Barrier to where the sugar ship lay moored, the unloading still going on. It was about a mile. But then hadn't he *swum* a mile to get clear of the Yusulu when they shot up Sergeant Matu? He could surely row it. His eyes glinted and inside he felt a sudden kick, the kick of small success, the feeling of hope. He had a plan, and now he could see how the beginning part of it would work out.

And for the first time in months, Kaninda Bulumba smiled.

The boat was at a small jetty. Its owner was bending into it, scooping out the water that over-loading brings. Such boats weren't only for fishing. In the wetlands along the shores of Lake Albert the small boats were used for transport – especially up and down the creeks leading to the villages and the inland markets. Cocoa, bananas, beans and plantains brought down, fish taken up. And people. Along the small rivers people even went to church by boat, some kids went to school.

The platoon was on its way to the rendezvous in the north. They were resting up on the shores of the lake, with thick rainforest at their backs and the open space of the lake in front. Look-outs were posted, but the platoon was in a good spot for not being taken by surprise. Now word had come that a cache of Yusulu weapons had been found in a village up a small creek. Sergeant Matu would go, to judge the weapons – they might be rusted and useless. But poling the boat needed attention to the water; other eyes would be needed to look for Yusulu, and crocs. In case the weapons were good, Sergeant Matu needed someone small and light to go with him, someone who wouldn't take up too much space.

Kaninda was chosen.

The boatman was neither Kibu nor Yusulu. In every war there are people caught up, from neither side. This man told Sergeant Matu that he was from the Ugandan shore of the lake, had come north from Lake Victoria when the Nile perch had eaten every other smaller fish and his living had disappeared: and being one of those who move about to chase a living, he was not easily going to give up his boat for the Kibu cause. He was sorry, he was in Lasai but this was not his war.

Sergeant Matu accepted the man's refusal, walked Kaninda away along the shore.

'Not the end of it,' he said. 'Cigarettes, perhaps.' Cigarettes were money. Two or three packets of cigarettes would be good payment for a boat for half a day. 'When he's off from the boat, you

untie it and wait for me upstream. Save time, you got me?'

Kaninda nodded. This was a simple task for a soldier.

He took a long way round and waded quietly through the papyrus shallows, as stealthy as a water snake, while Sergeant Matu went back to the man. Coming closer, Kaninda saw the sergeant crouch on the bank and offer cigarettes, in the barter position of no threat. The man crouched, too, took some. Then there was talking and nodding, and he went with Sergeant Matu to where more cigarettes would be.

This was the moment. Kaninda came out of the reeds, up to his chest now in the muddy water. He swam to the boat, three fast strokes. It was tied at the front. He tried to get his fingers into the wet knot; but there were no scissors in the Kibu army, no clippers like at 14 Bulunda Road, everyone chewed their nails – how could he get his fingers into the tight hemp? So how did the boatman manage? Then he saw: the end he freed was secured at an upright, and this was shackled with a padlock. Rope into chain into padlock.

Try as he might, he couldn't pull the staples from the wood. With all his strength he tugged and twisted, but he wasn't tough enough. He'd been picked for a special mission and he couldn't do it. Of all the boys in the rebel platoon, he was the one to be picked, and he was the one to fail.

He went back to the boat end, tried again to loosen the knot, went at it in a panic with his teeth. But it was wet, slippery, hard. If he'd been a boy with any tears left in him, he would have started crying now. He was a failure.

A whistle through the teeth and Sergeant Matu came walking along the bank, alone. 'No problem,' he said, and with a swift slash of his American buck knife he freed the boat.

'It was too tight.'

'Then cut. No knife, no soldier,' Sergeant Matu said. But he didn't sound grudging; something had gone well.

'The boatman said, "Yes"?' Kaninda asked.

'He's content.'

And the mission went as planned, with a pile of good bolt-action rifles at the end of it; but Kaninda vowed he would never go on one such again without the proper tools.

So he would need a knife. This little boat bobbing on the Thames was tied with blue sisal, stiffer to untie even than rope, but there were many sharp knives in the kitchen at Mrs Captain Betty Rose's...

The long plan was laid. But first there was the Yusulu revenge to come, when Theo brought N'gensi to the river. *Then* he could say in a dream to his father's ghost that these things were going well.

He left the river, took the road way back to Wilson Street. It was the way he had come from the school in the midday, through factory streets where huge vehicles were lined, the jack-knife sort with six sets of wheels. He read from their sides where they came from, all over Britain – Liverpool, Manchester, Glasgow. Looking up at the cabs, they seemed miles high, with curtains behind the seats where the sleeping bunks were. He had seen these at Lasai Port, on a walk with his father when they had seemed good fun, like riding the North South train.

But the warmth coming off them, the smell of the fuel, was just army to him now; not a Sunday walk any more but the transport of war. Fighting was his new life.

He came round a lorry after crossing the road, went past the front of a hot engine. Looking along the pavement he saw a girl at another of the cabs. She was in a short skirt, looking up; and she lifted a foot to the mounting plate and pulled herself up to see in through the cab window.

She hadn't seen Kaninda, so he stepped back into the road out of sight. He guessed what business she was on, and he didn't want to be seen seeing it. She was the sort of girl who made drivers feel happy a long way from home, and one of those drivers might not want a kid in the street to know about it.

He counted a hundred, slowly, accurately, Sergeant Matu accurate, without speeding up: on a mission you had to know a second from a racing heartbeat. Then he counted another hundred, and looked out – to see the girl coming closer.

It was Laura. Laura in make-up, looking twenty years of age, in a leather top and bare open neck, not wearing the gold cross she always wore.

He came out.

'Kaninda!' But she didn't look ashamed, she stared straight at him, not like Laura any more but like someone else. 'I know what you're up to.'

He waited, looked her in the eye.

'You're going to do a run. You're on your toes...'

He narrowed his eyes at her, didn't understand that.

'You've got a plan – lucky you!' And suddenly her arms were round his neck, she was squeezing him hard, holding on, her body shaking and her eyes crying hot wet tears down into his shirt – this girl who had grabbed him before to save his life.

So he held her tight, hard, let her cry. He thought of Gifty in trouble, of his mother on the day her father had died, when he had been the only man at home as the news came. And he thought of himself, and how long it had been since anyone had held him so tightly and he had felt their warmth. He had held the wounded, they had held on to him; but now he was holding a girl, and suddenly it was something he wanted to keep doing for ever.

He couldn't say anything, but his lips were kissing the tears on her cheeks.

'No.' She pulled away. 'I'm sorry.'

He looked at the ground.

'I don't know what I'm doing, where I'm going, what I was up to, running off, too. See, I've...'

'Troubles, you got?'

'Yeah, troubles I got. I was...I'd better get back...' But his face must have told her what she looked like. 'Can't go like this, can I?'

From his pocket Kaninda found a Mrs Captain Betty Rose tissue, and stood in the lee of a lorry and used Laura's own tears to clean up her face.

Helping the girl who had saved his life.

CHAPTER TWELVE

Theo Julien could talk a clam open. OK, he'd had no success trying to sell a sight of Kaninda's bullet wound – but ninety-nine times out of a hundred a bit of brilliant patter would get him what he wanted. And the deal today was, get Faustin N'gensi down to the Barrier.

Which was not so easy – given that Faustin was being 'minded' by teachers all the time. This might slacken off as the next school crisis hit, but before nine and at breaks right now he was watched in the school yard like a Category A prisoner taking exercise.

However, pos-it-ive, everyone has to pee; and when Faustin went into the lavatories Mr Long waited outside – so as not to let Kaninda in at the same time. But others could go – and in the lunch break Theo felt the need just when Faustin did.

He was a wiry, quiet boy, Faustin, who wore his school uniform like a city clerk's, not like a soldier's on manoeuvres. His long fingers were more the pianist's than the commando's and in Lasai he carried a briefcase, not a gun.

'Hey, Foz, man, you on your own?'

Faustin was washing his hands but checking in the mirror. 'Teacher...' He turned to the door, looking ready to run if he had to, or shout.

'Not on your own here – on your own where you live. No brothers an' that?'

Faustin shook his head.

Theo was at the urinal, hands occupied, making himself no threat. 'You phone home, do you, like, Africa? Or ain't you got no one to phone to – that's why you're here, sort o' thing?'

'Have a sister...'

'Yeah? Where? In London? Wi' someone else?'

Theo didn't bother with washing his hands. He came over to put an arm round Faustin's shoulder, best mates, walked him out of the lavatories and gave Mr Long a wink on the way downstairs.

'Somewhere, now.' Faustin shrugged. 'Lasai convent school. We split up.'

'Tough, man. Like, I had one an' all, a sister. Once.' Theo flicked his fingers, goodbye. 'Same as you – I don' know neither...'

They had come to the ground floor door into the school yard. 'Only, Mal, my brother, he runs – no, he don't run it, he works for – this phone shop in Deptford. Y'know – cheap calls to the Caribbean, an' Nigeria, Ghana, where you come from...'

'Lasai?'

'Yeah, all that. Sort of, if you wanted to get in there to phone places, like your missing persons, Red Cross, convents, put word out about your sister – long calls an' not ritzy priced – I reckon Mal can swing it. Or fax. Pos-it-ive.'

Faustin looked at Theo hard, before twisting his head to look around the yard like a nervous bird about to feed.

'Only, I don' suppose your ol' lady where you're living gives you the run of the phone, eh? See, it all helps my brother in the slack time. Worth a go, i'nt it?'

Faustin swallowed, a telling movement of his Adam's apple.

'Tell you what, come over my place tonight an' I'll give you the rip-off. Then it's down to you.'

'What place?'

'Where I live. Down the Barrier Estate, not far.'

Faustin frowned. 'You can't bring to school?'

'No, you gotta talk to Mal. He does the deals.'

Faustin thought about it. 'OK,' he said. His eyes took on a faraway look, like someone trying to see across continents. 'Good.'

'Meet you my place. Pioneer House, anyone'll tell you. Half six.' Theo walked off, found Kaninda in a corner. 'Game on! Good pitch, man, say it myself, 'cos he wasn't gonna be into "smack", was he?'

'Not about Crew you told him?'

'Neg-a-tive. Found out about his sister from a kid in his class.'

Waiting in the Barrier underpass Kaninda heard the slap of the water against the river wall as a launch went upstream. There was no other river traffic in sight, and no one else seemed to come here: this was no popular public place like Flamingo River Park in Lasai City. No children played on the swings and ropes so far from their flats, and each time Kaninda had been here he'd been alone with only the people he knew: it was good for a killing. The water was low, the tide running out – the force of a fall would be broken; but then N'gensi couldn't swim, could he? It would still be the finish of him.

And coming along the path from the Barrier flats were two figures; both boys, both black, one walking straight, the other jigging round him like a soldier who's sat on an ants' nest.

Kaninda kept himself back in the gloom of the underpass, made slits of his eyes because whites shine: he wouldn't catch N'gensi if he took off from there, he had to wait until the enemy could be grabbed. He inched back even further as he heard Theo rattling on.

'Mal's gotta be here in a minute. Seein' a punter in the Barrier, then comin' out 'bout quarter to...'

He could lie as glibly as Sergeant Matu telling a prisoner he was going to be let go.

'Jus' down here...'

In the shadows of the spring evening, Kaninda could see Faustin N'gensi's face, looking like a man ready to make a break for it, not so trusting...

'Through here, Foz. Pos-it-ive.'

But an underpass gives no options to run off to the side. A metre short of it, Faustin stopped like a suspicious buck – as Kaninda came leaping out of the shadows. 'Yusulu!' He came fast with his arms out straight, grabbing for a hand-to-hand throw – a fierce grip on the shoulders, a kick sideways at the legs, and Faustin N'gensi was on the pathway under him, prone for the jump up which came crashing down with a knee in the groin. A hand off one shoulder, a hold on the face and the Yusulu head was pulled up and cracked hard down on the concrete.

'Jesus, Ken!' Theo stepped back, away from this onslaught. 'Screw this!'

Kaninda heard nothing, saw nothing but the hated face of N'gensi with his mouth open, half knocked out. There was no resistance: it was just get the boy up onto the rail and over into the river.

But there were two days to go till Saturday. He wanted no witnesses to this; witnesses could be forced to talk. 'Go!' he shouted at Theo. 'Go – or you, too!'

Theo backed into the shadows. 'I ain't here, man, I ain't here!'

The boy still groggy, Kaninda hauled him to his feet and pushed him to stand against the river railings. A hand at the neck, one under the crutch, a lift and – over! Down into the running tide. But—

'I'm here the same as you!'

N'gensi was coming-to. The surprise of it stopped Kaninda for a moment.

'*Not* the same as me! I'm Kibu, you're Yusulu.'

'And both no families.' The boy could hardly get out the words with Kaninda's grip on his throat. 'I'm not a fighter. You can...kill me easily. But I'm still...the same as you...'

Kaninda's hand went under his crutch for the lift. 'OK no family. And why?!' Lift the Yusulu up ready for the roll, never mind him trying to punch. Why should he listen to pleading for mercy; little Gifty had pleaded and shouted for her life before this boy's tribe had fired with those smiles on their faces. Now Kaninda tried to find a killer's smile from somewhere, but not so easy somehow with the boy's words in his ears like the echo of gunfire. 'Enemy! Yusulu!' A new determined hoist, getting N'gensi along onto the flat of the wooden railing.

'I didn't start it! You didn't start it...' It was a throttled pleading and a last violent but weak struggle like a fish in his father's hands.

'Neg-a-tive, Ken.' Theo had come running up again. 'Got enough blood on my 'ands already, I ain't dancin' to this rap.' And he pulled Kaninda away from Faustin, who crumpled onto the pathway.

So, Theo! Kaninda coiled for an attack on the traitor, panting, spitting the blood wet of hate onto the ground, as Faustin got to his knees, to his feet, and found the strength in his legs to run from the pathway.

'Sorry, Ken...' Theo blocked Kaninda's way, backing off fast, palms up in pleading, and got just enough distance between them to turn and run, Olympic fast, towards the Barrier estate and his flat.

Kaninda dropped his hands and watched him go, breathing like a fighting dog at the end of a kill; except he hadn't killed. And like that he stood, unrevenged, and cursing Theo and the Yusulu.

The United Nations soldiers didn't know who was who. In the blue berets of the peacekeepers they'd come into the north from Sudan and right now a patrol was fanned out behind a white armoured truck, moving north-south down the main arterial road. The UN was trying to be a buffer between the Kibu and the Yusulu, but they couldn't tell one side from the other; they weren't up with the racial differences – and both sides wore the same camouflage khaki uniform, where they had it.

Kaninda was back off the road lying in a natural hollow, not much cover, but to have run for it once the UN was in sight would have made him a surefire target. They had their AK74s at the hip, and eyes everywhere serving as ears, too, because armoured vehicles are 'deaf' from the noise of the engines; and so are those around them. He was two days away from hearing Sergeant Matu and the platoon being shot up and was the only Kibu soldier alive in Lasai so far as he knew.

But some of these UN soldiers had a name for being quick to shoot and ask questions after; some-

times led by officers who didn't speak their language too well. It was always someone else's war to them, so why should they wait to get shot?

Perhaps it was the recent killing of the people Kaninda had fought with, perhaps it was the food he hadn't eaten for two days – not even able to steal from a soft village after it had been burned by the Yusulu – but he was shocked, light-headed, not knowing where he was going or what he would do, lying in his hollow for the UN troops to pass; and he forgot Sergeant Matu's constant warning: 'Soldiers on the road are showing you what they want you to see, just... It's the rest you look for, you get me?'

And now one of the rest got Kaninda. He'd come at him through the sparse cover, as stealthy as a striped hyena. And with Kaninda lying flat on his stomach, watching the patrol, there was no knowing the boy hadn't got a grenade there.

The click of the safety catch had Kaninda rolling over fast and grabbing at the soldier's leg. Stupid! He should have put up his hands. The muzzle was at him, but it was the jumpy eyes that told him what was going to happen.

'Hold your fire, soldier!'

The man just held his fire, but didn't move his finger a millimetre on the trigger, didn't blink his eyes in his watching of Kaninda.

A corporal from the UN patrol ran over from the road.

'Get up, fellah.' Now two muzzles were aimed at him. 'Hold 'em high!' The man's automatic did the jerking demonstration.

Kaninda stood, put up his hands, and the corporal gave him a quick frisk, all that was necessary for a skinny, hungry, tattered kid.

'Where you from?'

Kaninda did his 'no-speak-English' face, showed his arm with the bullet hole in it.

'Kid's been shot,' the corporal told the private, who still wasn't going to blink, not while Kaninda could pull some stunt. Kids did all sorts in civil wars like this. 'Take him back to the Dodge, give him to the Red Cross.'

The Dodge was a big open truck coming a hundred metres behind the advance patrol, with old men and women bumping and swaying in it, and a group of convent girls with torn blouses and shaking, bloodied legs: all looking pathetic; the refugee prisoner look.

Kaninda was taken to the truck and pushed up into the back, straight off sitting there looking like the rest – under the eyes of watchful guards who'd shoot if anyone tried to dive over the side.

And it was now that it hit him. That the running was over for him, and the fighting part of his war. He'd been captured or rescued, whichever way he wanted to think of it, and he'd be put in a secure compound with these others, these sad victims of the war, these non-fighters he'd despised, not to take any more active part. But at least he was alive. Just now he'd been saved by someone putting a stop to his execution.

Back at the house Laura's new rebellion came out in the open. Before, it had been secret, but tonight she found how words can run as strong as any tide and take you with them.

'Where's that boy gone again? Gettin' to know London?'

Laura didn't answer. He wouldn't learn much about London from the world atlas he'd taken from her shelf. Captain Betty Rose was pushing into the jacket of her uniform, donning the Lord's colours for the Thursday night 'Silver Bells' choir and band practice. 'He's out an' about worse'n Felix the Cat.'

Laura was still in her school stuff, not going anywhere much in the sloth of her depression, worn down by her mother going on about Kaninda between praising God by getting her voice in trim.

'All hail the power of Jesu's name, let angels prostrate fall...'

Well, this one had fallen flat on her face, Laura thought. Prostrate, down and out, abandoned, hopeless...

'He don' say a lot, does he? No name for anyone, not even "Mrs". No "please" or "thank you" if a nod or a grunt will do...'

Laura went on saying nothing.

'They teach English in their schools, it's what they speak in their business, it ain't as if he can't speak a bit of language to us. I know if I was plucked by the Lord from that camp in Lasai I'd want to say a few words of "thank you"...'

Laura was suddenly carried before the torrent. 'Well, if you didn't go on so much he might just get a word in edgewise!'

Captain Betty froze with her belt unbuckled. She gave Laura a look she might have saved for Satan. She started three different sentences but clearly didn't know what to say. No one – not her husband Peter, not God's Force members, let alone her daughter Laura – had ever given her a sharp answer like that.

She got there, though. 'Are you sayin' I talk too much?'

Laura was at the door, ready for the slam out; she

hadn't wanted to get into this, but she was in it now. 'About God you talk too much!' she said. 'If you talked to the boy about himself, or to me about me, or to anyone about *real life* you might find someone talking back to you!'

'God in Heaven, hear this!'

'See what I mean?'

'What you sayin' to me, girl?'

'What I said!' And Laura did the slam now, got out of the room.

'And where you goin'?'

'Where I want!'

'It's "Silver Bells"!'

'Stuff "Silver Bells". Ring 'em yourself.' And Laura ran along the hallway and out of the house with another mighty slam. She was still in her school gear – white blouse, black skirt, white socks, flat black shoes – and no key, no coat, no hope.

Crying now, she took herself through the streets to where she knew Kaninda would be, somewhere along by the river where he always was: because tonight she needed to find him: now her mind was made up about what she was going to do.

And he hadn't let her down. Unlike God and her mother, it seemed he *was* there when she needed him – right now along the Thames Path watching the twenty-four hour unloading of a sand ship.

Sand crunched underfoot; spillage from the overhead conveyor sprayed over the pathway, an Asda shopping trolley leaned against a fence, and in the mud of low tide others lay on their sides.

But Kaninda was studying the sand ship, although not standing there quietly like an observer; he was breathing heavily and he had some sort of a dry scratch on his face like a line on a slate. The black parka Laura's mother had bought him was scuffed and rumpled. He looked like a kid who's been in a fight.

'You had a fight?'

'Always fight.'

'Who with?'

Kaninda didn't answer, but turned away to the sand ship.

'Not going to throw yourself under a mound of sand, are you? Suffocate?'

Still no answer.

''Cos if you are, I'll come under with you...'

Kaninda suddenly turned back; and did what he hadn't done before; not for Laura, not for anyone else. He showed an interest in someone else. 'You tell me.' But he didn't lean on the riverside railing, or sit on the concrete slab of an old quay; he stood to attention to be told, as if he were taking in military information.

And in a blurt of tears and sobbed words, Laura told him, it all came out. She started with Theo and his brother's car, she told about Dolly Hedges, and she ended with the insulting of her mother in the house. And all through her telling ran a mix of guilt for the little girl and anger at God's letting her down.

Kaninda didn't ask any questions: there were no questions to ask; she told him everything. He could have been a Catholic priest in a confessional; he could have been a magistrate in the court, everything came out.

At the end of it, he sighed. But he put a hand on her shoulder, then held the two hands that had saved him from going over, down to his death. He looked out at the suck of the tide, where the mud was shining in the glint of the setting sun.

Laura released her hands, found a tissue, dried her face. She was suddenly calmer now, Kaninda's hands could have been the hands of some sort of healer.

'This ship's no good...' she told him. 'See the name? "Sand Cardiff"? Sand comes from Wales, not Africa. This ship goes in the wrong direction.'

Kaninda didn't frown – he understood what she was telling him. Part of it. Instead, his eyes looked down river to Tate and Lyle's wharf, and Laura's eyes followed too.

'I've made up my mind,' she told him.

Now his eyes narrowed.

'When you go off on your ship, on whatever tide...'

Already his face had become a mask.

'...I'm coming with you.'

And the two of them could have been sculptures, they stood there so long.

CHAPTER THIRTEEN

Kaninda led the way back to Wilson Street, his mouth firmly shut. *This Laura coming with him*? He'd had his life saved by the girl, as he'd had it saved by the UN corporal, as Sergeant Matu had kept him alive a hundred times – and he was grateful, but he was a soldier getting back to his war; he could not be distracted by someone else. The girl had her troubles, but she would make his own a thousand times worse if she tried to go to Lasai with him. Where there was room for one to hide in the belly of a ship there might not be room for two. He knew how to be a spirit in ghosting in and out of places for food and drink without being caught – she would never know about that. And if she ran away from England, wouldn't these people here start a worldwide search – when they wouldn't care a Lasai shilling about him disappearing?

But she had seen what was in his mind – she *knew* his Africa plans because he had stupidly looked across the river at the sugar ship – she was as sharp as Sergeant Matu.

She was just keeping pace as he walked fast. 'You ready for World War Three when Mum gets in from "Silver Bells"?'

'Always.' He walked on, faster. She had to run. And she wouldn't keep up when he was on the trek north from the ship. But for now he would keep his mouth tight shut. Slack words could breed trouble like aedes mosquitoes.

'She'll want to know why I was rude about God. It'll be like Judgement Day.'

So? He hurried on. Keep moving. Action was better than words. If it was his mother – which Mrs Captain Betty Rose was *not* – she would come at him from an unexpected quarter. Instead of telling his father to speak to *this boy* with a switch cut from the banana tree, she would cry that she was being a failure with him. But tonight Kaninda would be in his room with the atlas, measuring distances, planning...

'You! Ken, uh? I want you here!' Not Theo shouting, although he was one of those present, but the man Baz snapping his fingers. It looked like a meeting of Lasai street kids sharing out cigarettes, six or seven of them sitting and leaning on the two smooth black canons which were set like statues in the paving. Their heads were down, as if no one wanted to be prominent to others passing by.

'The Federation war...'

'Yeah!' One of them – all older teenage boys, black, white, Asian – spat on the ground with relish.

'...I'm calling up the Crew.'

This Baz looked like a man who liked to be obeyed. To have the boy Theo sitting quiet and respectful told the story of his power. Kaninda stared at him. Their war was still not his, whatever initiation he had passed to get at N'gensi. He was ready to walk on to the house.

'An' you're one of the Crew I'm calling up, uh?' It was not like a question but an order.

'Yeah, Baz, he's in. He's hot, this man!' But Theo was not on his feet, he was tailing off, staring at Laura, who was catching up. He was staring at her being with Kaninda.

'Well, that's good news. Good news.' Baz came over to them. ''Cos if this "hot" man blows out, it won't be me he's letting down, it'll be all the Crew – him bein' a member...'

Kaninda stood looking easy; but he was always ready for the swift strike; hands by his sides, space kept from sudden attack, his weight on the non-kicking leg so his boot could have its full and heavy swing at the groin. Still he said nothing; he was not promising more than he had already done. Not for anyone.

Except for the girl who had saved his life.

''Cos it wouldn't be him, not just him who suffers, uh? Next o' kin, that's where we hit traitors...'

Baz's face was close to Kaninda's now, because he had come forward and Kaninda would not back off. And Kaninda knew about next of kin suffering; wasn't that how information was got from village prisoners who claimed they knew nothing of Yusulu soldiers? But he had no next of kin. His next of kin were dead now, and eaten by animals.

'No, it wouldn't be just you, Ken – you let us down an' we cut the girl.'

Kaninda's face felt cold, the cold of his contempt. As cold as it had been said. *The girl*?

'Lor!' Theo was on his feet – a look at Laura and a step towards Baz. 'What you on about, man?'

'I'm on about winning this war. No one comes on my estate an' kicks-in the likes of little Jackson, do they? No-one comes down the Barrier an' takes the piss out of me!'

'Too right, Baz!'

Gobs of resolve hit the paving.

'So you be sure, sunshine.' Baz had come back at Kaninda. 'You're in – or she's *ugly*!'

Kaninda went on staring into the man's face. He could see how clever this Baz was being. As well as knowing she had pulled him back from going down to his death, he also knew that Laura was Theo's girl, so he was putting the threat on him as well.

And although Laura could think that she would not be there, that she would be on the sugar ship soon, Kaninda knew that she would not. She was not coming with him, so if he didn't act as one of their clan this Crew's revenge could still be carried out.

'What problem?' he asked, shrugging, like Sergeant Matu at the captain. 'What problem, just?'

He was in.

'Right.' But Baz Rosso was stopping any slaps on the back for the boy – because *he* was the main man. 'We gotta get the rest – you – ' he pointed at Theo – 'get razzling at school tomorrow, I want everyone called up.'

'Sure, man.'

'An' round the flats we'll knock up every Crew who's ever been.'

There were nods and more gobs, and cigarettes

being passed among the troops.

'Only thing is – when?'

'I got football training, Friday...'

'Stuff it! When we go is when we go – right?'

'No.' If Kaninda had to be in, he had to be fully in. '*Where*, first.'

'Where?' Baz asked the others, this was so stupid. 'Down there. Where d'you think? Their streets. Pay 'em out where all their people can see they don' mess wi' Crew.'

But Kaninda was shaking his head. 'Not there. They know, there. All the places, their hiding, the best ambush...'

'Well, I know down there an' all, uh? It's only through the town...'

Now Theo was on his feet. 'Or here then, man – eh? We know our patch. We can skin 'em down our Barrier, an' over into the Mississippi. Pos-it-ive!'

Kaninda had looked away, thinking. 'Through your town.' He crouched, like Sergeant Matu using a stick to make a diagram in the dirt. Others crouched with him, except Baz. 'Start there, just, where they live, only *some* men. Pretend, run off, back through the town, an' they come after. The others –' he waved a hand at the Crew – 'ambush!'

They all thought about it. 'Down the town?'

'All them people?'

Kaninda nodded. 'Best. People help, rebels always attack at the market place.' He tried to find the word. *Machafuko*.

'Confusion!' Theo guessed.

Kaninda's eyes opened. 'Confusion wins!'

'I can see that,' Baz Rosso said. 'Divide an' rule.'

Which was not the same thing at all; but for Laura Kaninda had shown them that he was worthy Crew; proving his value as a real soldier. He knew: in Lasain market places there were children, old people, bags and carts, laden bicycles, fright and surprise – they all helped the attacker, the ambusher who waits beside stores, under stalls, behind heaped goods. And escape is easier, afterwards.

'Yeah, that'll be it,' Baz Rosso said. 'So, that makes the "when" an' all, uh?'

They all looked at him. 'How come, man?'

'Saturday. Forget the snooker. It's Saturday, when everyone's down the town, in'it?'

At which Crew fists clenched, smiles spread, hearts raced, and spit boiled. And Baz Rosso grabbed Kaninda's belt and pulled it off-centre to the right.

'Saturday, sweetheart. Saturday's the day!'

Queen Max had read about coma victims being

played their favourite music, having pop stars or footballers come to visit; well, for little Dolly there was her, with news of the revenge war. She was in Jenner Ward. They had moved little Dolly out of Intensive Care, since all they could do now was wait, and talk to her. She was drifting in and out of being with them, but things were looking up – although she wasn't saying any more. There were no broken bones, it had been a glancing blow, the injury had been the crack to the head on the kerbside. So all the talk was going on – talking to her, activating the brain.

'How is she?' Queen Max asked an orderly.

'She comes an' goes, love; but comes as much as goes. Still says "white" over an' over. I sing her 'Colours of the bleedin' Rainbow' to change the record, but she still says "white".'

Queen Max leant close to the pinched little figure, lying still on a plastic pillow, hardly making a dent in it. 'We'll do 'em Saturday, love, we'll get them red car filth. Accident and Emergency'll be full to overflowin' with Barrier Crew Saturday night!'

And she went, nicking a fun-size Mars from the nurses' counter; going quickly and wasn't there to see Dolly come-to again and hear her take in a snorting breath and growl, 'White!'

*

Kaninda hadn't known cold. At home in Katonga, being high ground, the weather all year round was not too hot, not too cold, nights as well as days. Jackets were worn for business, not for keeping warm. There was no fire in his house nor a place for one, except for cooking.

But he knew cold here in London – outside when the sun had gone down and inside tonight where Mrs Captain Betty Rose was acting like refrigerator coolant. He knew the reason so he wasn't surprised by the chill, but Lieutenant Peter was, because he soon found some of God's work to do on a jamming door back at the headquarters.

'Silver Bells' practice was over – without Laura's bass drum – but her mother had not taken off her uniform as she normally did, getting back to the house. She kept it on, even the cap, like making a strong presence of God's Force until bedtime; chewing her mouth on words she didn't speak as Laura took Kaninda into the sitting room and turned on the television. But at least Judgement Day hadn't happened.

'This'll tell you about London,' Laura said. '"London Bridge", good programme.' She said it in the sort of voice Kaninda's mother used when she and his father were planning some birthday treat, it wouldn't have tricked his chameleon. She shut the door and against the sound of the television she started talking, fast.

'Did you see those trolleys near the sand ship? In the mud and on the path?'

Kaninda had seen them.

'They're from where the seamen push their beer and food down from the supermarket – then they can't be bothered to take the trolleys back...'

Kaninda looked at the TV violence of a police arrest on an estate like the Crew's; all acted for the cameras. He shrugged at Laura. So?

'Provisions. *We'll* need to take food, the sort of stuff the ex-army shops sell. And water.'

Kaninda turned, eyes narrow as scratches on ebony. His plan was to survive the first twenty-four hours on a small pack of stolen fruit and some bread, then start stealing from the ship's cook. And there would be plenty of sugar...

Laura was whispering on. 'Those places that sell uniforms and boots and camouflage tents, they sell iron rations, and water tablets. I'll get some tomorrow...'

Kaninda said nothing. He hadn't seen such shops, but the rebels had captured ex-US army iron rations when they overran the Batama Fort. They were dried, needed water, but Kaninda had eaten some 'chocolate' and been sick. Only Sergeant Matu seemed to thrive on it.

'And we'll need plastic bags for...what you have to do...'

Kaninda's eyes opened up a bit. She had thought about this carefully. He had known long-hidden snipers get fouled out.

'And cough medicine...'

He was impressed. A cough could give a hiding place away.

'Cough medicine keeps you drowsy. The boat people escaping from Vietnam took bottles of cough mixture to help them sleep through the long voyage. The sort with sedative...'

'I keep awake!'

'...and in the bottom of the bottles they hid rings and jewellery, to bribe the sailors. Do you reckon – ?' Laura looked at the ceiling, towards the bedroom above where her mother would have her rings.

'No jewels.' Kaninda came from a diamond mining area. 'You have jewels, they kill you, throw you in the sea. Why not? *Your* diamonds, *my* diamonds.'

Laura nodded, accepted that like a partner, changed her tack.

'Why were you at the sand ship tonight?'

'I look...' he said.

'For the sort of places to hide? I've thought about that. We'd be suffocated by raw sugar, but if it's going back in packets, baled-up, there'll be loads of nooks and crannies. If not, where the crew lives, we'll have to get down between the ribs of the keel under there, where they keep stuff they don't use much.'

'I find a place.'

Laura leaned her elbows on her knees, watched the television without seeming to see it; finally looked across at Kaninda.

'What time do we go?'

'In the dark.'

'We row to the ship...?'

No response.

'...we climb the rope...?'

He was back to staring through slits. One person climbing the rope and slipping onto the deck – one trained fighter – that was OK, just. But two, when one of them was this Laura, who knew nothing of how to be a spirit ghost... 'We hide,' he said. 'On top. Then...' He scuttled his fingers along the arm of the chair. 'In...like rats.'

'Yeah, rats.'

Kaninda was uncomfortable. The less you said of plans, the better for the operation. He went to get up from his chair, but she stopped him with a hand on his arm.

'Do rats go up to Heaven?' she asked. 'Do you think?'

He didn't know. *She* was the girl from a Bible house. One thing he hoped – that Yusulu did not. He couldn't bear to imagine the dead enemy in the same place as his mother and father and little Gifty.

Whether or not Yusulu went to heaven, before he stowed away on the ship Kaninda was going to send N'gensi *somewhere* in the other world. It still had to be his aim, whatever the boy had said at the riverside. But in school the boy was guarded tighter than the Katonga mine chief after the collapse of Deep Road Nine. Also, Theo would not be able to trick him to go to the river again. So Kaninda knew that the execution would have to be unarmed with one of Sergeant Matu's dojo attacks, or with a knife from Mrs Captain Betty Rose's kitchen. But it would be done – although not done too soon, because he would be the first to be suspected. He had to make the attack on Saturday, the last thing before he went. He would find where N'gensi lived, which would not be far from the school, he would go there; and he would trick him to his door. Then...

For a soldier like Kaninda, finding where Faustin N'gensi lived was easy. It was a matter of tracking him after school ended for the day. This week N'gensi was being taken home by a teacher, or three or four older students. All day Kaninda had been waiting to be interrogated about his last attack on N'gensi, but none had come, the boy had said nothing, probably from Yusulu pride. But he wasn't too proud to be escorted home like a chief.

Today was Friday. Theo was going about in the breaks talking to boys, carrying out his orders from Baz Rosso. Charlie Ty was walking about with a swagger, and the word that could be heard in the yard and in the corridors was *war*. There was an atmosphere in the school like at Katonga High the morning after the entombment. The teachers knew something was happening, and in the classroom Miss Mascall kept her eyes all round. Even so, she couldn't stop Kaninda from being allowed to go to the lavatory just before the end of the afternoon – from which he didn't return. He walked out of the school gates and waited across the road in the space between two office blocks.

When the rest came out, N'gensi was with three bigger boys and a girl. Did they know Kaninda had disappeared? They could do, because their eyes were all about them like the armed guards outside Lasai City shops. They were being very careful at first – but Kaninda followed easily; and after the first streets the escort relaxed keeping eyes all round for attack; they just walked either side of N'gensi and talked about their own things.

Kaninda got very close – to keep up his skills. For a tracker it was always keeping someone in the street between you and them, and many pupils were going home. As the main street was left behind and they walked down a side road, parked cars gave him cover – nose to tail like a metal hedge. As Kaninda guessed, N'gensi's home was not very far; students did not come to school here from all over the district. And in five minutes the escort saw him in through his door and left him.

And left Kaninda staring in surprise at the place.

It was a street restaurant, a place of steamy windows and small tables and chairs; and painted on the glass was: *'Jesus Saves' Tea Room – all profits to the Lord,* and underneath in smaller writing were the hours of opening – *8 till 8.*

Kaninda rubbed at the old bullet hole in his arm, it had started tingling. This was better than he had thought! If he came before eight o'clock tomorrow evening he could go inside and ask for N'gensi; he would not have to call at the door, waiting on the outside. He would be inside and more than halfway to the enemy before he realised; and be down at the river before the Yusulu's body hit the floor...

He turned away, still being careful not to be seen.

...Then, alone, he would get to the sugar ship. Certainly, alone; he could not be slowed or exposed by the girl: and she knew nothing of what happened to such females in the camps.

But first he would repay his debt to her by playing his part in the London tribal war.

CHAPTER FOURTEEN

Lying in tepid water Laura stared up at the glass bowl of the bathroom light, clear again, the steam gone. This was one place where there was some privacy in the house, where she was allowed to lock the door – so Saturday morning or not, she stayed in there till her fingertips puckered. Her chin on her chest, she lay and looked down at herself. Her figure was a woman's but she felt like a stupid kid. She was making no ripples on the water but inside she was churning with frustration. What you saw in life wasn't what you got. She *hadn't* meant to do anything bad – just be a bit rebellious with Theo – but it had made her into a wicked sinner who'd never get to Heaven: her mother said so: anyone who'd done that sort of thing didn't stand a chance.

But, so? Laura slid down and up in the bath, made a wave now. God had let her down badly, hadn't He, *badly*; He'd shown her He wouldn't want her in his heaven anyway. So now all alone she was carrying a guilt so strong it was going to take her away from here.

And away from all this, she thought. Here she had light and heat and dry towels, downstairs there was a fridge and all the other electrical stuff, and all over the house there was central heating. Her mother always said they lived in luxury because they lived where there was running water. And what was she changing this for? A long journey with someone she hardly knew, on the way to fighting in some other country's war: sleeping rough, washing in puddles, eating food even her imagination couldn't taste. She'd be living on their side with violent soldiers – or she might get captured, with *certain* rape and a terrible death from torture or Aids. Or she might just be bitten by a mosquito the minute she got there and die from malaria: her mother had taken all sorts of tablets when she went.

That was what she'd be swapping for what she had here – out of desperation at what she'd done and her mother's ramrod attitude. And that last was the worst bit; that was the clincher, worse than the God thing, even: because her mother used to have a bigger heart than that. Before she got ordained she'd been so different. She'd been religious, OK, but not fanatic. She'd been fun, and cuddly. In her head Laura saw the picture of her mother in the park playing football once with her and some boys. A ball had come over and she'd whipped off her glasses and headed in a great goal. The kids had gone crazy, and she'd run back down the pitch going 'Yoop! Yoop! Yoop!' and waving her arms. And at home she'd sat with Laura on the settee and told her tales of life in Victoria, Mahé, her Seychelles home: of Tante Los and Money George and island hops and beach barbecues and land crabs clacking in the night. Good memories, which made today's hell all the worse...

Laura slid further down in the water, pushed her head back till it went under. Could you drown on purpose? If she opened her mouth wide and forced her body not to come up, could she finish with everything here in the bath?

And then *definitely* never earn a place in Heaven! She came spluttering up, took in a quick deep breath and sat rigid. But hold on! *Earn a place in Heaven*? Wasn't there another way to get back in God's and her mother's good books? She'd got to get away now, she'd decided that, but what if she went to Lasai with Kaninda but didn't stay long with him – if she went off and found a refugee camp to work in, did good things, became something like the Florence Nightingale of Africa? Wouldn't that make up for what she'd done? *Good works in the field, the same as her mother had done going out there*? If she earned something like that, couldn't she get the Almighty to see things differently and give her some hope? After a year of sacrifice and danger, couldn't she come back to England as a new person, couldn't she come back home reborn?

Splash! Yes! That was a better way of looking at things: more hopeful. Because that gave her something to aim for, didn't it, something pos-it-ive, not just running away, but going off as part of a proper plan: paying for her crime through a harder life than young offenders' prison would ever be.

'You gone down that plughole in there?'

'No.'

'Then you comin' out with the "Silver Bells" in the Town Centre?'

'Not today.'

There was a sudden angry rapping at the door. 'Well that ain't the way to wash your sins away! It's a clean *spirit* the Lord wants, not some blaspheming teenager on the further side of a locked door.'

Laura heard her mother clump off down the

stairs. She'd made *teenager* sound like the worst sort of sinner. Which she was. No, there was no other way; she had to go with Kaninda tonight and make her new plan work: which meant she had to make sure his plan worked too.

Like a Rank Xerox Kaninda's brain had photocopied that page of Laura's atlas. If the ship put in at Maputo he could say by heart the townships he'd pass on the track north: Manhica, Macia, Chókue, Mabalane, Mapai – and then over the border, up through Zimbabwe. But if that thin line he'd seen running up the map meant railway he could hide in a freight truck and get himself north faster and easier, much. He had helped sabotage a government train on the Sombamba stretch when Sergeant Matu had no explosives, when the men had uncoupled the last trucks and sent them derailing at the bottom of the slope; so he knew the slowness of a heavy train going up, how easy it was to jump on. 'Right, right, right, you get me?!' He could hear it being said.

A loud slam of the door downstairs told him that Mrs Captain Betty Rose and Lieutenant Peter had gone. 'Silver Bells'. When he had eaten his breakfast the woman had said he was welcome to go too. 'No, I read,' he had said. And she had given him some easy stories of Jesus. But it was the map he had read hard.

Now there was a silence in the house; until a door clicked at the top of the stairs, at the bathroom. He knew the sound of it. Some time he had to get down to the kitchen, to choose the knife he would carry that night, but he would not make his move yet. He had learned from Sergeant Matu that under cover in villages you stole what you wanted at the last moment before needing it; if you were caught, you were still innocent till then.

He wished that Laura had not quarrelled with her mother – because now Mrs Captain Betty Rose was looking at her all the time, being suspicious of her. *Normal* was how he wanted the house to be, because when eyes are sharp for one thing they're sharp for everything: the Yusulu soldiers rounded up were not always those the patrol was searching for. And he wished that Laura had gone with her parents instead of being here, waiting to be a plotter with him.

After the door click it was like waiting for a timing device to go off. Fifteen, fourteen, thirteen, twelve, eleven...

'Kaninda!'

She was outside his room. He went to the door and opened it, neither wide as if to a partner nor narrow to raise her suspicion. She was barefoot, wet hair, in a dressing gown. She had come direct.

'This war...'

'Which?'

'The Crew. You don't have to get sucked into that. Don't forget, I won't be here for Baz Rosso to retaliate; nor will you. We'll be on that ship...'

'I still go.'

'But it's happening in the town. *They're* in the town!'

'It's the plan—'

'Them, Mum and Dad – playing with the "Silver Bells".'

Kaninda stared at her, through her. He shrugged, and wanted to shut the door, but he didn't want this girl to know his deception. 'But *you* don't go there,' he told her.

'I've got to; the iron rations...'

'No iron rations. Food is OK.'

'But you mustn't get hurt or caught; we mustn't miss that ship.' She looked at him, head just on one side.

He looked at her. She was powdery from the bath, smelt of balms. Her eyes were not red today but clear and big. Her bare feet beneath the towelling dressing gown looked small, unprotected. Alone in the house with her, just for a moment, he wanted her to unwrap that towelling and take him inside it, for the feel and the comfort. If she had shown him the tip of her tongue again he would have done so himself.

But soldiers kept to duty or they died going soft.

'I go to the Crew.' He had no watch; he looked round at the clock on his table.

'I said, you don't have to go.'

He shook his head.

'Then you be careful, boy soldier. You're my ticket to a better place.'

Which Kaninda did not argue with; and in any case, it was best now to shut his door.

'We carrying?' Snuff wanted to know.

Queen Max gave him a look. 'Why get tooled up if you don't carry it?'

Snuff's gun was pink, Charlie Ty's blue, facing the screen of Time Crisis III and shooting at the enemy as the seconds raced away. Taking up all the machines in Mega Arcade the Fs were looking occupied; but the real business was the gang briefing. While the cash assistant turned his back, saw nothing – on a promise from Queen Max – she was going round giving out cans of Kwik Spray for hair.

'Wha's this?' a tasty John wanted to know.

'Share it round. Hair dust, different colours.'

'Wha' for?'

'We're all red, blue or green heads, then, Doz! Till you brush it out quick. If Old Bill gets involved it cocks up the witness statements. 'Long as you sling the cans first, don' 'ave 'em in your pocket.'

'Yeah.' The big fellow looked round at his mates on the Daytona Rally. 'You fancy me ginger?'

Queen Max slapped him round the head, hard. 'This is Federation war!' Over the sounds of the arcade she told them all. 'Any tools you use, you lose before you get nicked, right? In the river, if you have to.' She looked round at them. 'But don' get nicked. This is for little Dolly – we *don'* want no prisoners an' we don' want no casualties. Right?'

'Yeah.'

Rally cars crashed out of control, skiers fell down precipices, laser crackshots were exterminated as their attention all stayed on Queen Max.

'The meet's at the Ropeyard Arms twelve o'clock – an' we march on the Barrier, along the riverfront.'

'Yeah!'

'An' don't no one not be there in their coloured hair!'

Charlie Ty looked at the can Snuff was holding. 'Ever seen a red-haired Chinese?' he asked.

'Only when it's fresh blood,' said Snuff.

And Charlie Ty nearly sniggered.

The Crew were out of sight down on the rocks, pretending to throw stones at a shopping trolley. They could have been any Saturday crowd of youth on the loose. Charlton Athletic was at home that day to Millwall, another local club, so there was plenty of youth starting to gather. If the police helicopter was watching out for trouble, it wouldn't be in Thames Reach town centre, it would be in Charlton near The Valley.

Baz Rosso sat on the river steps, giving the orders.

'No weapons!' he said. 'We're goin' in the town, uh? Anyone carrying's not gonna last two minutes, they'll have us on video an' get the law down. Hoods up an' use your boots – it's a good kicking we're giving 'em.'

'*Nothing,* man?' Theo asked. 'Not my eighty-mill mortar?'

Baz Rosso looked at him, bent to the rocks and picked up a smooth stone. 'One o' these in your fist, or a bunch o' keys. But nothin' you can't drop without getting sussed, or what you couldn't have in your pocket legit.'

The younger Crew started looking round for the right sort of stones.

'So how we gonna know they're coming?' someone asked. 'If I'm in the doorway of the DSS, how do I know you've got 'em chasing you through the town?'

Baz Rosso smiled, the great leader. He fished in his pocket and pulled out a mobile phone. 'Courtesy o' Mal Julien,' he said.

'Don' spread it, man – he don' know!' Theo warned.

'I got one, an' he's got one.' Baz pointed to Kaninda, who had been standing silent against the river wall. 'He's your man to watch for. When he gets word I've got 'em coming, he's gonna give the signal.'

'How?' They looked at Kaninda; who put back his head and gave his best Sergeant Matu jackal shriek, the one that fooled the other jackals. It was loud, fingers in ears.

'Then you wait for 'em to pass an' come out of your hidin' places...'

'An' *'ave 'em*!'

'Sure thing. An' 'ave 'em – hard!'

'But don' smash them new Nokias!' Theo warned. 'Or it'll be me havin' it hard!'

With his back to the wall Kaninda looked at the Crew – all with their belt buckles to the right, all in their hooded T-shirts – wearing the symbols of their army and as raw as Kaninda Bulumba when he'd been recruited from being a Lasai street kid. But they were fighting for their clan pride, so he knew their spirit.

And he would help them all he could – for Laura – before he left this city to get on with his real war.

CHAPTER FIFTEEN

Laura came out of the house. There was somewhere she had to go, something she had to do before she left Britain for the new life – she had to speak to the girl who might have no life at all, new or old. She had to confess.

The hospital stood on Matchless Hill, which ran from the lower end of Millennium Mall up to Windmill Common at the top, well away from where the 'Silver Bells' were playing God's tunes. Its view of the river, the Dome and the London City Airport was matchless; that is, for those who could see it. What Laura didn't know was what state little Dolly Hedges was in for seeing or hearing anything.

But she wasn't about to find out straight off; because as she turned out of her front door to go up Wilson Street someone called her name from across the road.

It was Sharon Slater, who was standing secret behind a plane tree; and in her hand, wrapped in newspaper, she had a number plate. *The* number plate.

'Sharon...' Laura stared at the plate.

'You want this, do you?'

'Why?' A try at bluff.

'My dad's doing up our room. He'll be into everything. I got some stuff down behind the bath, but I can't lose this nowhere...'

Laura's heart was picking up a faster beat. This wasn't some blackmail, was it, at the last minute before she went? 'Why do you think I want it, it's not mine.'

'It's your *business*, though!' Sharon's face took on the expression of her stepmother, that look that said 'You're guilty as hell, my girl.' *Knowing*, was the word. 'There's a war on about all this today, an' I'm not bein' seen slinging this in the river, thanks. But you can, if you like. Else...'

Laura didn't wait to find out what else. 'Give it to me,' she said. 'I'll get rid of it for you.'

'No – you get rid of it for *you*!'

'Same difference.' Laura tried to seem above all this nonsense, tried to look the God's Force Junior leader who carried a bit of authority around here. She had a plastic carrier with her – she *was* going to pick up some stuff for the stowing away; there were things girls needed that boys wouldn't even think about – so it didn't have to be seen. If she couldn't do it before, she'd lose this number plate in midriver when they rowed down to the ship...

'See you,' said Sharon.

'I doubt it,' Laura couldn't help saying. But if it meant anything to Sharon, the girl said nothing.

Just filed it away as one of her secrets, probably.

Like a Roman legion they followed Queen Max out of the Ropeyard Arms car park. No one in the pub had taken much notice of them gathering outside; nothing was ever noticed by Ropeyard drinkers other than the drinks in front of them: no Sky TV, no machines, no interest.

The river walk was signposted as an urban footpath to Greenwich, passing through the Barrier Estate; but no one much walked it. No one much *walked*. So for the Fs it would be this unobserved short cut along the river side of the town through to the battle that was on. The Crew might know they were coming, but they wouldn't know what hit them. This wasn't just for kicks, this was for grudge as well. Car windscreens would be put in, petrol poured into lock-ups and set alight, flats' windows smashed and most vital of all, the Crew was going to be clubbed or kicked or cut – because the Crew wasn't hard the way the Federation was hard. They tossed around with initiations and off-front buckles, they lived on a new estate that was the pride of the borough and they came from all over the world instead of the solid backstreets of Thames Reach. The Crew were nothing.

Queen Max was in the shortest skirt she could find, her belly was bare and her shoulders shone with body rub. Her hair was blue to match her eyes and her face was ugly with its hard beauty twisted up with hatred. Her boots were long black lace-ups, her hands were free, but she had a Boss bag on her back, fifteen inches long with a fourteen inch butchers' knife inside it.

And inside the Federation was Dutch courage lager, and more than a few snorts.

The chant started as they widened out at the promenade that ran past the town centre.

'Kill! Kill! Kill! Kill!'

A seagull bombed towards them and turned away tighter than an RAF Tornado.

'Kill! Kill! Kill! Kill!'

The Barrier was still half a mile away, but the hyping up was always vital. Behind the three leaders – Queen Max, Charlie Ty and Snuff Bowditch – came the other older hards, about twenty of them; then the fourteens and fifteens, girl Feds among the pumped-up boys, and at the tail the Federation's little soldiers, the 'in and outs', the kids who ran in, chivved and ran away.

'Kill! Kill! Kill! Kill!'

But Baz Rosso and the Crew weren't waiting for them at the Barrier. Up river the police helicopter fluttered over Charlton with its binoculars trained on the Millwall firm but this small contingent of the Crew was heading east towards the promenade.

'Hey, man, listen!' Theo jigged in front of Baz Rosso.

'Uh?'

'Liss-en out!'

'Kill! Kill! Kill! Kill!'

'They're comin' through... So?'

'But we was supposed to get there first, start it down the Ropeyard...'

Apart from Theo no one broke step, they marched on towards the Federation, chanting.

'Don' matter, suits us better. Not so far to run 'em.'

'Yeah! Pos-it-ive!'

Someone picked up the Federation's words. 'Kill! Kill! Kill...!'

'Neg-a-tive, man! Mu-ti-late! Mu-ti-late! Mu-ti-late!' It was a faster rhythm to march to, got them there quicker.

The Crew decoy took it up. 'Mu-ti-late! Mu-ti-late! Mu-ti-late!' Baz Rosso was leading, the Nokia in his hand, the number for Kaninda already in, just waiting for the 'send' button to be pushed.

And now they could see them – the Federation coming on behind Queen Max. With the town centre on one side, the river on the other, the two gangs came to within thirty metres of each other. An old man sitting on a bench looked this way, then that, and drew up his feet onto the seat, as if his departed wife was hoovering.

'Kill! Kill! Kill! Kill!'

'Mu-ti-late! Mu-ti-late! Mu-tilate!'

Queen Max put up an arm and called a halt. The F was tattooed in her armpit.

Baz Rosso called a halt, too.

'Brave arseholes!' said Snuff. 'There's only ten of 'em..'

But Queen Max was frowning. 'This is some stunt...'

'What stunt?' Charlie Ty asked. 'Couldn't raise a flag, them, leave out an army! They're just showing out, gonna run away an' think they've got it all over with...'

Queen Max stared at Baz Rosso – across thirty

metres and back six years. Her eyes said she was someone not about to be fooled.

Except, Baz Rosso was *Il Duce* of wind-ups. He knew how to get people going. 'Left your vest at home, Max-*eene*?' he called; giving her name the long drawn-out whine of derision. 'Or did you leave it in some ol' codger's car, uh?'

She stared back. Someone behind her spat. Weapons were being twisted in sweaty hands. Any second now...

'Or is Ty an' Bowditch fightin' over who's gonna wear it tonight? Still padding out your bra wi' Tampax, are you?'

That was it. Showing the F again, Queen Max suddenly brought her cleaver from her bag and led the charge at Rosso and the Crew.

'Kill!'

But the Crew didn't run yet. They stood their ground till the Federation was near enough to smell blood, and then, '*Scappare*!' Baz Rosso yelled, and the Crew turned and legged it, not back towards the Barrier but off the promenade through hedges and flowerbeds and into the town.

'*Kill*!' And the Federation came after them, an army of coloured heads chasing a scatter of hooded T-shirts. Within seconds the only one left on the promenade was the old man, clutching angrily at his knee where he'd been kicked by a ten year-old.

The Crew ran hard, up into the town. From the doorway of Chappel's Funeral Shop Kaninda saw them coming; heard them before the Nokia warbled at him.

The High Street, leading in from the river, was a walkway – with a Galloping Horses roundabout, an ice cream van, the Millennium Mall where all the main shops were – and today, further along, the God's Force 'Silver Bells' playing hymns. Busy, and normal.

But not normal now was the Federation gang coming running. Kaninda saw a big fierce blue-haired girl at their front coming up on the Crew decoy close enough to start swinging at them. There was the Chinese from the school yard looking red and violent; the others bright headed and hard eyed like tribal warriors. The Federation clan was being sucked in. Sergeant Matu would have had a chasing force coming in behind to pick off the tail runners and stop them turning and running when the ambush hit; but the Crew didn't have the troops, and Kaninda had to wait until the Federation's main force was firmly in the street. He could see Baz Rosso running on, looking over his shoulder, ready to turn and fight in the canyon of the shops; and he could see that the Federation chasers were suddenly not sure that they wanted to come into the town like this. The big leader girl put her machete into a backpack, looking about her. But they were here now, and they suddenly decided to be violent all around them. A woman in their way fell and her cheap shopping rolled over the paving.

'You little toe-rags!'

Children on the roundabout looked down at the chasers and must have thought it was Saturday fun, till a small boy was punched on the leg by someone chasing, and fell off. Then wide eyes turned to wide mouths at his screaming and the chant of the gang – 'Kill! Kill! Kill!'

So, now! Kaninda threw back his head and gave the second jackal shriek that was the signal to attack. And straight off, from doorways, behind tubbed trees, the back of the ice cream van and off the Galloping Horses itself the Crew came fighting – direct at the enemy, not giving anyone time to swing what they had in their hands, getting in for close combat with fists and chops and kicks and head-butts, hand-to-hand street fighting.

There were screams and shouts and swearing. Parents yanked children back behind them, lifted babies in their buggies into shops, adults scattered, disorganised, had no way to stop this riot. The man on the Galloping Horses got on his mobile phone, the ice cream van was switched off, Captain Rose ordered the band to push their instruments into their cases and get into the shops. But Kaninda was aware only of the fighting.

It was toe-to-toe violence, and the buzz and bubble of it showed on the thugs' eager faces. For them nothing hurt right now, blood and snot and spit was just stuff to be got off the face out of the way. If they lost their footing they'd be kicked into unconsciousness unless someone got them up, but they knew that – this was all about risk and the thrill of it, where hatred and violence gave some purpose to their lives. It was for that – and for the pride of the tribe.

For Kaninda it was what he'd been trained for, what he'd done all year, except today he didn't have his M16. It was dojo fighting – roughened up for real combat. He chose his target quickly, went direct for Charlie Ty – because taking out a leader drops morale like the sinking of a stone. But through the affray he suddenly saw the flash of Ty's blade. His eyes sharpened on its edge – point up and it's coming for the stomach; point down and it's coming overhand for the chest.

Point up – under hand; the Chinese was trying to keep it hidden but he was running at him fast; no matter the twisted face and the shout, it was the force of the blade to worry about. Kaninda didn't turn, didn't run, he let him come – and at the moment for the knife to come flashing up, he jumped his feet one behind the other and threw his forearms crossed across his body to block the blow at the attacker's wrist. The sudden force of it stopped the Chinese and sent him staggering back, when before he could get his balance, Kaninda's boot had gone crashing into his groin, doubling him up to take the next boot full in the face – what Sergeant Matu called *juicy-juicy*! That was the Chinese.

Kaninda turned elsewhere. There was no thick of the fight because there was no thin. Everyone was in and hacking and kicking and punching and clubbing – but the Crew was without weapons and couldn't keep the advantage of the surprise ambush for long. Kicks couldn't counter clubs; punches and head-butts were no good against sharpened coins coming into faces: even with stones in their hands and keys between their fingers, the Crew were fighting at a different level. Baz Rosso had got it wrong; he'd underestimated the violent intent of these troops.

Rosso had gone for the big girl – leader for leader. She was at his hair while he kneed her groin, all along the turning step of the Galloping Horses; but others were going down. Kaninda saw what the Crew needed to do. Disperse.

'Pull back, just! Away!'

'In here, you's!' Theo heard him and started running across the paving and into the open glass entrance of the Millennium Mall: where there were shops and levels that could give cover and ways of escape. 'Come on, man!' – he dragged Kaninda in.

Some of the others went with them, but some didn't. Some hadn't heard, some didn't want to, some were lying bleeding on the High Street paving, and some were running away, back towards the river, chased by Federation the way lionesses chase the slower deer.

And it wasn't just the fighters running. The scared, strained faces of shoppers couldn't believe this violence hitting their High Street; they ran, huddled, took refuge in shops, dragged children legless, pushed grans and grandads ahead of them, shouted for the police as it all skirmished on, as shop security guards came running and a police car at last sirened through the street. At the sound, the Federation dusted their hair colour out, their weapons clattered to the paving and clubs took last swings at shop windows. They ran.

And now wounds started to hurt. Noses knew they were broken, tongues found sockets empty of teeth, fingers went to ears that had been bitten, blood gobbed from mouths and cuts down on to the paving, and in and out of sight bruises grew. Worse, without victory to lift anyone, there was a spitting, disgusting feeling of shame in the air.

But it wasn't all over. Theo and Kaninda had been seen going; a gang of four Ropeyard youth had seen the two boys run into the mall.

'Kill!' They came walking in fast, violence on their faces, past the open shop doorways where people were crowded. Theo ran for C&A, Kaninda went for Marks and Spencers; but he'd chosen a shop whose glass doors had been shut against the riot, and when he turned, the gang of four was walking in at him, gathering speed and force, ready for the attack – no weapons that he could see, but their boots were heavy and their fists were knuckled white.

'Kill!'

He could fight one, he could fight two; if he was lucky, he could get a chance at three because he knew where to chop, how to use his own hands like weapons. A finger jab at an eye could have it out of its socket; a chop at the throat could kill; speed and aggression were worth another man to him. But four! Numbers would defeat him, you had to have good strategy to win when you were so out-numbered.

And right now the first came at him, sideways on and telegraphing the kick. *Come on, kick*! He could ride it by jumping backwards and go for the off-balance enemy; his only chance was getting in among them where he could do more damage. But his back was to the plate glass of the shop door, and there was no jumping anywhere; he just hit his head hard on the window – and the first kick came and caught him where he'd caught the Chinese.

''Ave that, you black scum!'

It doubled him, nausea at his core, his body's reflex a doubling up. He couldn't see for the red pain, he couldn't order a muscle to his own defence. In the agony he fought it but couldn't stop it, his head lolled helplessly forward for the chop, his face set up for the next hard kick. And while people stood, people stared, no one moving to help him, here it came...

But no, the next move was from a uniform, wading in among the attackers and giving out some of what they were about to deliver.

'Get off! Get packin', will you!' Punches, slaps and a good kick. And with that example others came to help, because this was God's Force speaking, this uniform was Mrs Captain Betty Rose, backed by her husband and two or three 'Silver Bells'.

The gang ran, the one she'd grabbed somehow twisting himself out of her neck lock.

'Kaninda Rose, what the hell is goin' on here? How d'you get involved in this riff-raff?'

Kaninda said nothing. He never said anything to her, much, but then at this moment he could not have said *Sir* to Sergeant Matu. He crouched down and cradled his hurt, took deep breaths and spat his sick onto the mall floor.

'You all right, man. Should've come wi' me. Pos-it-ive!' Theo had returned.

'What you doing, what's goin' on?' Captain Betty still wanted to know; but now she was addressing Theo, who might be able to tell her.

'We're down here for a look around an' we're only in the middle of this mash-up!' Theo looked up at the big woman. 'Ding-dong, vi-o-lence, I hate that stuff!'

Kaninda was still looking at the ground, heaving in breath. But what had she said, what had she called him? Kaninda *Rose*? Out of her mouth like that, in her quick talk? The supremity of it! But the Sergeant Matu guts! She'd done what no one else had done. She'd gone for them as if she really had been his mother.

'Kaninda, you better get home with me. All this conflict an' all.'

He stood slowly up.

'Yeah, man, we better get home,' Theo persuaded. 'We don' want no more of this mayhem...' And with an arm round him, he walked Kaninda away. 'He'll be hunky wi' me, Mrs Captain...'

Outside the mall, it was quieter of movement; but the talk and the crying was loud enough. And an ambulance was sirening through, while overhead the police helicopter had diverted from the football and was hovering.

Kaninda looked round without twisting his head. Baz Rosso had gone, but a security guard in uniform and two women police were taking the blue girl leader into the mall, off the street. She had a bag on her shoulders, but between its straps her skin was cut and bruised. She was bright red with her hair down over her face. She walked with them, talking about being jumped, and not so much looking like a leader now as a loser in the gang warfare.

Painfully, Kaninda walked home. He had done what he had said he would do. He had taken a bad kick, but he had paid his debt to the girl Laura; Baz Rosso would not punish her. One target had been taken. From now on he had just two: to settle his war with the Yusulu in London, and to get to his ship to Mozambique.

*

Laura put her head round the ward door. It wasn't a children's ward, there were beds for six in this partitioned area – and the other five were women, three of them sitting out in chairs and staring at her as if she were a woman from Mars. But there was no mistaking Dolly Hedges. She was the wispy little one whose name had described her in Laura's head. She was propped up on pillows, asleep but breathing quite heavily, and there were no tubes, no electrical gadgets, nothing beeping.

'She's better today,' one of the women said.

'Ate some breakfast,' said another. 'Little mite.'

'Talking some more,' the first one added.

Good news! 'So she's coming out of it?' Laura asked.

'Oh, yes.' Matter-of-fact.

Everyone watched Laura as she drew out Dolly's chair and sat on it. She wanted to take the small hand, but she didn't dare touch her; her hope had been that Dolly would be able to hear the confession she had to make, but whether the girl could hear it or not, now the moment had come a nervousness rolled in Laura's stomach like Seychelles surf.

'Dolly...'

'You can talk to her, love.' It was a nurse. 'She's

been talking to us, yes, Dolly? *And* she's changed her record at last.'

Laura twisted her head.

'One more word, but the rest will come, sure as anything.'

Dolly hadn't woken, but the nurse wasn't showing any concern about that.

'What...was the new word?' The first word had been vital enough. Sitting there, Laura didn't know how she managed to ask it, but there was the question, coming out.

'"Van". "White *van*" – that's what she's telling us. Must have been what hit her...'

Van!

Laura turned back to stare at the sleeping child.

Van?

And inside, as she sat there looking at the peaceful face, all at once her Seychelles wave became a calm, clear ebb on a silver beach: as clarity suddenly came to her; as Dolly's new word suddenly let her see in focus the events her trauma had fuzzed in her mind these past days.

Van. Yes, the white van! The van that had come out of a side road and cut in front of them while she'd been concentrating on steering straight. Theirs hadn't been the only car on the street that day; of course it hadn't. In her head all she'd been seeing was the girl running out, when Theo had grabbed the wheel, swerved and bumped them as she looked in a panic for the brake – and the next thing was, the girl was in the gutter in a heap. But in her guilty head it had only seemed *the next thing. She could see it now, the white van that had come between. It had cut her up and been in front first along the street. It hadn't been their car that had hit Dolly, it had been the van – they'd hit the kerb – and with the van having no-windows how could the little girl even have seen through it to call Laura Rose 'white'?*

It was there; at this instant it was crystal clear in Laura's head – and she had to freeze it, remember it.

'Dolly!' she said.

They'd been stupid, she and Theo *could* have caused some terrible accident by the criminal thing they'd done. But they hadn't actually done it. Laura took a huge breath and blew it out. 'There but for the grace of God...' didn't they say?

The grace of God! Laura straightened up, stared round the ward. They still deserved to be punished for it, punished hard, but the ringing, singing clarity in her head right now was suddenly bringing her the greatest news of all. She had been given God's grace at last; she had had to wait, but with this news now she could make her peace with Him. Even in her mother's eyes she had not been so wicked that she couldn't go to Heaven one day.

She bent over and kissed Dolly on the cheek; and quietly, slowly, but inside wanting to dance out of the ward like the start of a musical, she went to the door to run from the hospital down through the Millennium Mall to the town centre, where she would go to find the 'Silver Bells' and take over from whoever was banging her bass drum.

CHAPTER SIXTEEN

Laura ran, her head feeling light at the guilt being lifted. She wanted to smile at people, bless little children. She'd been stupid – a rebel, a sinner, if not as wicked as she'd thought – but now she could earn herself a place back in the fold. Her mother had no reason to disown her, she didn't need to run away; she wasn't one of those who didn't deserve to Heaven some day.

At the top end the Millennium Mall was busy and normal. This was the higher level that ran along to become the first floor, with a lift and escalator down to the ground at the lower end. But the quicker way was to run direct down the side slope. Beneath the light of the angled glass roof Laura darted between shoppers, under rotating mobiles of Easter bunnies, past the AA, didn't do the lottery, wasn't going into the Southern Bank for credit. She'd got her credit back; her credit in the eyes of God. Everything was dreamy.

But down by the escalator there was a buzz around, a throng, like bystanders not wanting to disperse after an accident. People were talking in clusters, everyone at once; shop assistants were at their doors staring out and about without blinking. Something had gone off and she knew what.

With a tight grip on her carrier bag – she still needed to dump this number plate – Laura wove her way among them all: to be stopped by the sight of Baz Rosso coming into the mall looking serious and intent on something; looking about for someone...

He'd threatened her yesterday, but his slight smile when he saw her said he wasn't after her. But she couldn't run past without *any* word – anyway, he might know where Kaninda was, and there was something vital she had to tell him.

Baz jerked up his fist in a small signal of victory. 'We showed 'em, uh?'

'The Federation...?'

He shushed her, went on looking around: so she could run on.

But what they'd said had been heard by someone coming fast behind Laura, spinning out of the Security office. Queen Max pushed into her in a lunge at Baz Rosso.

'Mind out!' Laura shouted.

'Showed *who*, tosser?!' The big blue-haired girl grabbed at Rosso, knocking Laura sprawling at the foot of the escalator, clattering her carrier bag to the floor and sending the number plate skidding out on the marble like a tray onto an ice rink.

G34 MLS.

'You!' Queen Max spun round on Laura, lying there.

Laura got to her knees, grabbed for the moving escalator to get away.

'Red car! You was in all this!'

'No, white van!' Laura was onto the escalator, on her feet, throwing up her arms to defend herself as Queen Max swung at her with a fist like stone, smashing into her cheek. Like the rag doll that Dolly Hedges had been before, Laura's neck gave, and her head cracked back on to the hard edge of the escalator.

'Christ!' Baz Rosso was onto Queen Max; Security came running at the screaming.

And while people stood, open-mouthed, Laura's limp, unconscious figure was carried up, up, up to the level above.

Number 128 Wilson Street was like a house in mourning already. Kaninda knew the tearing in the stomach, the shrinking in the throat, the tightness in the brain, of such tragedy. When the Yusulu soldiers had left his house he had stood in shock for maybe half a day, there in the bullet riddled living room of number 14 Bulunda Road. That was what Lieutenant Peter was doing now; standing, staring, his eyes big and his face as white as that wall.

Mrs Captain Betty Rose had done differently. She had wailed and ranted and cried and called to the Lord in His mercy to save Laura, to give her back to them. And now, as they both got ready for the hospital, she sat in a chair and she cried into her hands. She looked smaller tonight and her voice was younger, more like a girl's, more like Laura's.

'I been so...stupid. That girl was into something, an' I never saw it. I been so...tied up...all in my own stuff.'

Lieutenant Peter couldn't move to give her comfort, to put an arm around her.

She suddenly looked up at Kaninda. 'I done good, haven't I? I brought you out to safety an' a good life?'

He stared, too.

'But I lost sight of that girl an' her needs...' And the woman sobbed and rocked herself there in the chair.

Finally Kaninda couldn't take it any more.

Lieutenant Peter was fiddling with his car keys, impatient to be away to the hospital, but so much inside his own grief he was still not able to come to his wife. So Kaninda went to her and touched her on the shoulder; his first ever contact.

And that was all. He stood away and went to his room. He opened and shut Laura's atlas, looked inside the front cover at where she'd signed her name. Already, the ink seemed faded, and he felt empty inside. The stupid, pointless way she'd come to be hurt! For what? Because there were tribes in London, gangs who wanted to fight, kids who wanted to pretend at wars: just as there are real wars that need never ever start.

But his own war needed seeing through. If he was to stick with what he had decided he still had to go to N'gensi's place, and then he had to get to the small boat moored up river, to put himself secretly on to the sugar ship. Because, why should this grief alter his plans? Laura hadn't been coming with him – although in a weird way he felt lighter about not having to deceive her any more.

There was a knock on his door. He slid the atlas under the bed. Lieutenant Peter was standing outside.

'We're going to the hospital now,' he said. 'Mrs...Tante...Betty is going to stay there till—' He turned away, came back. 'You can come with us and I'll bring you home...'

Kaninda looked up at him, shook his head. 'I will stay,' he said. He gave no reason, no excuse. Sergeant Matu said, 'Never offer more than you've got to, just.' So Kaninda didn't.

'I don't know how long we'll be.'

Kaninda nodded. For ever, that was how long, so far as he was concerned.

They went, and Kaninda had the house to himself. Now it was easy to put his pack together; the fruit he wanted, a bottle of water, and a thick jumper from Lieutenant Peter's cupboard – and from the kitchen, the knife he needed. There was plenty of time to choose.

The knife was not just for Faustin N'gensi. To a soldier a knife is more than a killing weapon; it digs holes, opens tins, cuts wood; it can cut free from entanglements. In Lasai, the rebels had a captured supply of American Buck M9s, ex-bayonet with saw-toothed back edges. In his stowing away and his journey up through Mozambique, Zimbabwe, and back in Lasai itself, Kaninda would need such a knife.

He found the best he could in Mrs Captain Betty Rose's kitchen drawer. Nothing there had a serrated back edge, but there was one short carving knife with a blade guard, and its shape told him she kept it well sharpened. All the same, he found her knife sharpening stone and put a killing edge on it for himself.

Finally, he stole a backpack of Laura's, and with the knife in the socks he had decided to wear, he came to the front door. There was one last look back along the gloomy passage – and he let himself out into the street.

It was half past seven and getting as dark as he wanted. The 'Jesus Saves' Tea Room wasn't far away, although he didn't know the way through the backstreets so he went to the school and on from there, the route he knew. Not far.

The lights from inside the café were already bright enough to show, a yellow shape spread out over the pavement like a picnic cloth. It was a corner site with the door on the angle between streets. And looking along one of them, Kaninda could see why it was busy inside – a few buildings away was a taxi place, Capital Cabs, and a line of old cars. He looked through the steamy window – and saw Faustin N'gensi sitting at a table near the serving counter, reading; it looked like several books at once, spread out.

Take time, take time. Too quick in, never come out! Sometimes Sergeant Matu would keep the platoon waiting till their muscles screamed. But he was right to do so. Kaninda saw what he wanted to see – several free tables, and one just by the door, no one seated there. He had to get in unseen if he was to have the drop on N'gensi. He waited some more, and as he had read the signs so it turned out to be true, a car door slammed and two men came walking along from Capital Cabs, money pouches slung round their necks. Kaninda pretended to be reading the menu in the window:

* All-day breakfast
* Egg, chips, peas or beans
* Saveloy, chips, tomato, peas or beans
* Cup/Mug of tea/coffee
* Buttered slice

But the men knew what they wanted, didn't pause, went directly inside.

Don't take the first table! Don't take the table at the door! Kaninda followed them in on the same opening of the door – and they didn't take the first table, they went further in. So he slipped inside to sit where it would serve him best, his head down as if looking at the text on the table. '*Man shall not live by bread alone, but by every word that proceedeth out of the mouth of God. Matthew:4.*' But all the time he was using the mirror of the window to watch the Yusulu.

The woman was bringing hot plates from the kitchen, calling out. 'Number seven!' She was younger than Mrs Captain Betty Rose, and white, and thin, must have lived by the words of her text.

'Over 'ere!'

Coming up from his books, N'gensi took the suppers to the man who had called. He saw the two new customers, looked up at the clock. It was ten to eight. 'OK,' he said. He glanced over at Kaninda, who showed him only the top of his head.

OK for him, too Kaninda thought. If N'gensi came to take the order it would be easy. A quick, hard, twist of the knife – and away out of the door. Already the weapon was in his hand. One lunge would do it, and Kaninda would be halfway to the river before anyone could climb over the Yusulu body in the doorway.

N'gensi took an order to the counter from the last two. Now he came over to Kaninda.

'You here for eating or killing?' he asked, standing over him.

It stopped Kaninda for that moment. He thought he hadn't been recognised; but he had, and still this boy had come to stand close. Close enough...

'I know what's under the cloth.'

A second surprise, when the edge was to have been Kaninda's; already the words had been in his mouth: *Top posho* and *sweet potatoes*, spoken quiet to bring him nearer for the lunge.

N'gensi didn't move, hadn't jumped away, wasn't running round the tables. He was standing, bravely. 'You think I killed your family? You think I blame you for my family?'

Now! Now! Do it now! But still Kaninda's hand was stayed.

'Yusulu, Kibu, Nyanga, Banyarwanda, Tutsi, Bakongo – tribal is political, boy. Them and us, you and me. But not really you and me ourselves – it's the leaders make it that way.'

Now, then! Still no one around was taking any notice of the quiet, calm talk from this boy in their own language.

'Number eight!'

Faustin N'gensi didn't turn. 'My family was killed the worst way. Atrocity. No mistake, boy, I hate, too – but I don't hate you. You are three hundred miles from me. Tribal war did it. War takes us all in its hand and smashes us on the rocks.'

'*Number eight*!' Still Faustin N'gensi didn't look round, and the woman took the plate to table eight herself. 'Friends!' she said. 'Why help when you can talk to your friends?'

Faustin stood his ground, his hands by his sides, the white shirt on his skinny belly inches away; the length of three knife blades away, just.

'I got a sister to find one day...'

A sister. Like Gifty – only *she'd* never be brought back.

'...Twin. Same age as me, went to Convent School, Christian...'

Like Laura. And like those girls in the UN truck.

'...but do it, boy. I'm not running from you for ever. They all commit atrocity. What atrocity is one more?'

Sergeant Matu had needed the boat badly if they were to go up river to the arms cache, that day when just he and Kaninda had gone to reconnoitre – when the sergeant had walked the boatman away with cigarettes and promises of good payment. The mission had gone well, and when they came back with the rifles he and Kaninda had carried them from the landing to the platoon by the quick way through the hyacinth weeds.

And Sergeant Matu had not cared what Kaninda saw – Kaninda was a soldier in this war, soldiers knew what things went on.

But Kaninda had been sickened at the sight. The boatman's head had been macheted with such force that it was no longer part of his body; such blows to the neck that the corpse seemed to have emptied itself of blood; it lay saturated in the mud hollow, where ants and mosquitoes were feeding already. It was like the atrocious sight of Kaninda's own family; and within the short hours the mission had taken, the smell had swollen to fill the air. Now Kaninda had added to it with his vomit.

That was atrocity. Atrocity is what is not needed to carry out a mission, to win a battle, to be victorious in a war. Atrocity is brutal, unnecessary – and that brutal killing of the boatman had not been needed. His arm twisted at his back and he would have surrendered his boat OK.

And Sergeant Matu was Kibu, on the just side – while the boatman had not even been Yusulu.

Kaninda did not know why. But he looked at the still and tense Faustin N'gensi and he gave him an order.

'All-day breakfast,' he said. 'Big, to travel on.' And the other boy went, while Kaninda bent to his sock and replaced Mrs Captain Betty Rose's kitchen knife.

It was rocky in the small boat when a craft passed, perhaps he should not have eaten such a good meal, even for free. But the food would sustain him for some time. Sergeant Matu forced them to eat sometimes when the journey's length was unknown, or the mission hard to forecast.

The knife would still have its use tonight. It would cut the rope and free the dinghy, rip open the canvas to let him inside the cover of a ships' lifeboat. It would shape the fence slats he had kicked out to serve as paddles.

And yet he sat there longer.

Faustin N'gensi was Yusulu, not Kibu. Even so he had been brave. He hadn't fought, he hadn't run, he had stood and *argued*. There were braveries other than fighting, and Kaninda knew that. He had been brave himself in not following the running Kibu when they passed his house, in surviving on the streets of Lasai City with the runaway kids before he became a soldier, in living the rebel army life in the camps. Perhaps this was because his father had always been brave, a Kibu manager for a Yusulu mining company, arguing that what he was doing was right; there were many who could not have held the position with respect from both sides. And hadn't N'gensi tonight sounded like his father, arguing a truth, as if talking quietly about this fish and that, when and where to cast the lines?

Was that why he hadn't killed N'gensi – his brave show – or was there some other reason to add?

A reason such as Laura – who had bravely

decided to come with him to Africa, to leave her family behind. Laura, who was the same as his own father in that tribal way: as his father had stood on Yusulu ground as a Kibu, she stood on Seychelles and English ground together; she stood on both black and white ground. Perhaps then she was the lucky one, she was the coming together of the clans, the integration. She was a new world person, perhaps. *This* new world.

That is, if she was anything – because now she was a victim of the stupid war between people here who did not need to war, who fought for the thrills, who didn't know the huge atrocity of real war.

Yes. Sitting in his cold, rocking boat, he saw that Laura was some of the reason. He saw her again in her robe, come from the bath. He felt her again hugging him tight and crying in his arms. He tasted again the salt of her tears when he had kissed her. He remembered her looking at him and flashing at him the tip of her tongue. And he thought of what had happened to her.

And perhaps it was this, perhaps it was together with those things that Faustin N'gensi had made him think about. The blade gleamed in the London lights – but Kaninda did not cut the rope that held the boat. He put the knife back into his sock and looked down river as the dinghy bobbed. The ship could go to Africa tonight – and it could go without him. He would let the Lasai war fight itself out – it would never, however it was ended, bring back his mother and his father and little Gifty. Revenge meant violence against someone soft and sweet like Laura.

Instead, he would go to the hospital to see her, and on the way he would take the knife to his home.

About the Author

Bernard Ashley is one of the most highly regarded authors in this country. Born in Woolwich, south London, he was evacuated during the war, and ended up attending fourteen different primary schools. After school, Bernard did National Service in the RAF where he 'flew' a typewriter. He then went on to become a teacher and later a headteacher – his two most recent posts being in east and south London, areas which have provided him with the settings for many of his books. Bernard now writes full time.

The writing of *Little Soldier* was triggered by television images of boy soldiers in the Zairean civil war, which moved Bernard to follow up with research in Africa and in south London schools, where there are many war refugees.

Bernard Ashley's other novels for the Black Apple list include the four books in the funny, gritty *City Limits* series, and *Tiger Without Teeth*, which was chosen as the *Guardian* Book of the Week shortly after publication.

TIGER WITHOUT TEETH
Bernard Ashley

Hard Stew punched him in the mouth with a fist like a knuckleduster.

'I want that bike, son, and that little smack's just for starters.'

Hard Stew always gets what he wants, but he's not the only thing chasing Davey. There's also a secret – the sort that jumps up on you and is more frightening than a hundred Hard Stews. The sort you've got to stare in the face. If you've got the guts...

'Bernard Ashley's greatest gift is to turn what seems to be low-key realism into something much stronger and more resonant. It has to do with empathy, compassion, an undimmed thirst for decency and justice.'
Philip Pullman in *The Guardian*

1 86039 605 4 £4.99

Also By Bernard Ashley

Drop in, hang out, meet the friends of the City Limits Café.

STITCH-UP

Will Dean lie for Sharon?

Dean and Sharon are an item. She's sharp, funny and beautiful. Her half-brother is sharp too – sharp and dodgy. So when a robbery takes place right in front of him, Dean has some heavy-duty thinking to do. Does his loyalty to Sharon extend to her brother? Or is this a stitch-up?

1 86039 481 7 £4.99

THE SCAM

'I've lost my Auntie Pearl!'

Mack's in trouble. His Auntie Pearl has done the bunk of her life, leaving him on his own. Can they find her before nosy neighbours get wind of the situation and rat to Social Services? Mack needs help, so his mates step in – after all what are friends for? Now all they need is the perfect scam…

1 86039 480 9 £4.99

Also By Bernard Ashley

Drop in, hang out, meet the friends of the City Limits Café.

FRAMED

'Watch out Mr Big, you're about to be framed!'

A famous face arrives at the City Limits Café – a TV face, the Big 'I am'. He commands attention and gives stick, which rocks young Lucy's confidence on stage and off. But Sharon's a natural at play-acting herself, and she's up to teaching him a thing or two.

1 86039 576 7 £4.99

MEAN STREET

It's no place to be…

A runaway puts Dean and Matt in a spin. She's a kid with attitude – a fighter, a survivor. Now Mack's having sleepless nights, and Dean wants to forget he ever met her. Kwai's kindness only makes things worse.
Can they – will they – help a kid down on her luck on Mean Street?

1 86039 407 8 £4.99

WEIRDO'S WAR

Michael Coleman

Daniel is known as Weirdo because he enjoys doing things at school that others think strange: working out mathematical calculations and formulas for everything, doing his homework and being on his own. Tosh couldn't be more different: hanging around with his 'friends' who use him as a butt of their jokes and picking on others, such as Daniel. So when they find themselves sharing lodgings on an Outward Bound weekend neither is too happy. And things can only get worse when they're involved in a terrible accident and become trapped underground together…

'Tense and psychological.' *The Times*

Shortlisted for the Carnegie Medal

1 86039 812 X £3.99

TAG

Michael Coleman

Pete and his friend, Motto are into graffiti...at first the raids are just a bit of fun, but the buzz is addictive and soon they are pushed into a confrontation with a notorious graffiti gang, the Sun Crew...

Changing friendships, gang rivalry, inner conflicts and a roller-coaster ride of a plot make this a terrific read, quite unputdownable.

'Coleman skillfully handles the change in mood from hard-edged tension to sharp poignancy, when Pete finally acknowledges the anger he feels about his father's death.' Books For Keeps

1 86039 654 2 £4.99

DAY OF THE DEAD

Anthony Masters

It should have been an exciting holiday in California...a rare chance for Alex to spend time with his globetrotting father. But Alex's father has other things to think about: a secret which involves black plastic coffins in the back of his truck and a trip across the border into Mexico – and he's not taking Alex.
But one way or another this is one trip Alex is determined to go on... And it will be a trip he never forgets!

'Anthony Masters is on his best edge-of-seat form' TES Primary

1 86039 657 7   £4.99

WICKED

Anthony Masters

Josh's elder brothers share a secret - a secret that is tearing them apart. Josh wants the truth...but is he ready for it? Is he prepared to find out that his brothers have turned bad, and that what they have done is truly wicked?

'Suspension is stretched almost to breaking point....' The Independent

1 86039 477 9   £4.99